The Weaving Of Threads

Book One

Lee E. Eddy

This is a work of fiction. Dialogue has been fictionalized and is based upon the Scriptures using the following translations:

The Literal Translation of the Holy Bible, third edition, Copyright 1995, used by permission of the copyright holder, Jay P. Green, Sr.

Name: Lee E. Eddy
Title: The Weaving of Threads/ By Lee E. Eddy
Identifiers: ISBN: 9781952369148
Subjects: 1. Religion
2. Fiction/Historical

Published by EA Books Publishing, a division of

Living Parables of Central Florida, Inc. a 501c3

EABooksPublishing.com

DEDICATION

To the people in the churches where I have been a pastor/teacher and the disciples I have had under my care, who have allowed me to experiment on them in ministry, I dedicate this book. You allowed me to work on things and delve deeply into practical application of the Word of God. Thank you.

CONTENTS

ACKNOWLEDGMENTS

It is my sincere desire to thank those who have watched me and helped me through this process. It has been totally unique to my experience to write a novel and the joy of it was inexplicable. I wish to thank Sarah, Carol, Miranda, Bob, and Roxie for their editorial work and in-depth discussions of matters that few have ventured to explore. Larry and Peter gave me invaluable insight and help in editing. All my other friends just put up with my joyous rantings and indecipherable musing. It was all with Jesus working hard beside us that we got anything done. For all of that, Lord, I am truly grateful.

CHAPTER 1
The Twisting of Threads
Jerusalem, 18 BC

He smelled so bad. The stench was nearly visible, like a cloud hanging about him. His own nose had long ago lost the battle and quit working. No one would let him come in to bathe because of the oozing, stinking sores. Lazarus had a life to be pitied. His life hung on by the thread of the compassion of those who passed him. But with the rank air about him, few came close enough to give him any alms.

Age and malnutrition took a toll on his legs. He leaned on a makeshift crutch to move a single step. Jerusalem afforded few places for him to find shelter, but he had to venture out to beg for food and water. He would cover himself as best as he could with his rags as defense against the heat and the scorn of the people around him. On occasion, his rags would lay too long on one of his sores and would scab over so when he moved, it would tear away, causing the sore to fester even more and ooze profusely. He tried to establish his own place to rest. But lepers would steal his meager shelters if he left them for any length of time. Fearful of contracting leprosy, he avoided them. At least his smell helped keep them away.

Though Jewish scripture made a way for the poor in the land to have provision, his immobility made gleaning almost impossible. His entire family was gone. Unwise choices caused him to lose everything he owned. The rich got richer, and he got poorer. Life grew worse when the Romans occupied the land. He could no longer pay the Roman or even the Jewish taxes. Then he got sick and his body seemed to turn against him. Now he was totally dependent on others.

The one hope he still had, though, was his faith in the coming of the Messiah. When He came, He would bring a Godly Kingdom. Every day Lazarus would pray. He would recite Psalms of praise. He had studied the scrolls when he was younger, keeping them in his heart and memory. Often these verses were his only comfort. "If only He would come today," he would think, "then Israel would be Godly again."

Lazarus was a young man when the Roman occupation began and Herod took his seat over Jerusalem. He had witnessed the beginning of the restoration of the Temple and the aquaducts that had been built. Life in Jerusalem had adapted, changing as they had to, but the one unchangeable thing—at least not to Lazarus, was the promise of God to live among His people in His temple. Faith in Jehovah was the foundation of their lives. Even at that, fewer and fewer people watched and waited for the Messiah. Synagogue life continued. The Temple was still the focal point of their well-protected spiritual lives. And political zealots and insurrectionists often made a stir. But few had faith in the coming King.

Lazarus clung to his faith like a shield. It was all he had.

He hadn't eaten for a couple of days. He was getting weaker. He had to get somewhere while he still could. "Lord God, please help me today to eat. I thank you."

Shimon wore his good tunic today. He was delivering the things he had made to his customers. Today was the day to deliver things to his richer clientele, so he had to look the part as one who served the upper class.

Shimon was a weaver. He had built his business through all the difficult times Israel had been through. He was nearing twenty when the Romans came. He had already started business as a weaver. He had apprenticed since he was twelve, taking over the shop years later when the owner was killed in a tragic accident at the ports of Joppa as he received cargo off the ships from Tarsus. When Shimon took over, he built the business and took care of the widow who had been left behind. With his wife dying and two boys to raise, his diligence and fervor made the business flourish.

Now in his late sixties, he gave more and more over to his older son to do the work, while he went out on deliveries and took in new orders. And this enabled him to be active and engaging. He spent much time at the Synagogue poring over the scrolls and having in-depth discussions with the men, always under the strict eye of the rabbis. Shimon was considered to be of the old guard. The new politics and movements of the zealots didn't interest him. He loved the purity of the Scripture and the Messiah they promised. He wanted everyone to walk in the ancient paths that brought peace to their souls. Everything else was a distraction to him.

God had blessed Shimon. His business always saw a steady stream of clients. They made lines of cloth from simple wool for cheap clothing to flax linen for more expensive clothing. He contracted with dyers, who would make the different colors for both thread and full cloth, and fullers, who would bleach and boil the cloth until it was pure white. Some of his workers just made the simple things, day in and day out, while he and his sons would work the higher-end cloth, weaving colors into stripes and patterns. Shimon was glad to get to the point where he could leave the shop and go out and mingle more with people.

Shimon considered it an honor to bless people less fortunate. Once a week he would go out with parcels of food and clothing. He couldn't get rid of poverty, but he could help. Some of the poor would recognize him as he went about town. He always smiled and spoke blessing on them. Most thought kindly about him, but they knew if they spent much time with him, conversation would turn political about the condition of Israel and the need to flow in the commandments.

He made his way to the portion of Jerusalem where the more affluent people lived, with packages bound up in twine. He carried beautiful light blue window coverings of fine linen ordered by a rich man he had known for years. This customer was hard to please. Shimon hoped he'd have no problems today. He steeled himself for whatever negotiation would be necessary. "Oh, Lord God. Bless me today. I need your help."

Lachish surveyed his courtyard from the balcony on the second floor. He was smug and satisfied with himself and his surroundings. He knew he ruled this domain with an unwavering hand like a personal kingdom. When he spoke, the servants rushed to obey. He considered every transaction as if he were conquering an enemy, taking ground, building his realm. He wore silks, satins, and fine linens with embroidery that couldn't be made locally. Today it was a flowing purple outer robe with a yellow under robe and red sash. He was most proud of his purple robe, it was extremely expensive and hard to obtain. He imported his clothing mostly from Greece and Egypt, with some things coming in from Rome.

He had made his money dealing with the Romans. He knew how to cater to their needs. He could get large amounts of meat, wine, and meal for the garrison in Jerusalem. If they needed something, they sent word to Lachish. He learned Latin so as to appease them in their own tongue. He would deal and double deal with the locals, taking a large cut of the transaction. He had an excellent grip on Greek, which was still the language of commerce in most of the world where he worked. He was Jewish and was raised in Jerusalem where he learned to barter. His father was one who would supply things for Herod, but Lachish found that working with the Romans was easier because the intrigue was simpler. Herod's court was a viper's den of back-stabbing, lying people jockeying for position. The Romans were simpler; you could see them coming a mile away. Everyone around Lachish considered him a traitor. They would still deal with him because he made them money. But he was not well liked, just tolerated as a necessary evil.

Lachish didn't care what the people thought of him. They were just rabble, the everyday folk of Israel. Some, like him, who lived in opulence, extracted what they could, profiting off the misery that had become life for the Jews. For the most part, though, he lived in his own realm, self-satisfied and arrogant.

Today he waited to do business with some of the lower class people he had to deal with occasionally. They were bringing in cowhides to be taken to the tanner, who would make leather for the Roman armor. The original armor came from Rome, but it had to be repaired locally. Most of his business was housed in a large building just outside of Jerusalem, but the negotiations of price and money exchange were conducted at his house. Lachish didn't trust people to handle his money. He preferred armed guards he paid very well to protect him. They would take him a couple times a week out to the warehouse to make sure things ran smoothly.

From where he stood in his villa, Lachish could watch the front entrance, opposite the courtyard. His guards were stationed in a room between the entrance to the courtyard and the front gate, where they had a small desk for simple transactions, and barred windows allowing them to see out onto the street. They were to screen and greet people who came. Lachish had determined the guards were to be obviously armed and dressed for action. One of the guards entered the courtyard, looked up, and bowed. "Lord

Lachish, a couple of representatives from the Sons of Debir are here to see you."

Lachish loved the power position on the balcony when people came. "Bring them in, Telem." Bowing again, Telem spun on his heel and went quickly out. Lachish remained there, to look imposing to greet his guests. Since he was somewhat shorter than the average man in Jerusalem, he used the height of the balcony to intimidate. He stuck both thumbs into the top of his red satin sash. He cocked his head back to appear to be looking down on them even further, his eyes looking out from under his folds of eyelids, sighting down his large, hooked nose. His obese face was framed with a sparse beard, closely trimmed. His cap covered his balding head and with the huge purple robe flowing around him, he thought he looked majestic. Telem ushered two men into the courtyard, then turned and stood by the entrance, watching them closely.

Both men came in, looking around at the very costly furnishings. Eventually they looked up and spotted Lachish standing over them. The older of the two smiled broadly. "Greeting to you, sir. Are you Master Lachish?"

"I am. And you are?"

"I am Uthai, and this is my son, Peretz, of the sons of Debir. We are bringing the hides as you requested." Both the men wore the common dress for the men of Israel, a short woolen tunic held at the waist with leather strapping. Their heads were covered in the common *keffiyeh*, a shoulder-length head cloth. The older man was more filled out, muscular, and work hardened. The younger man, Peretz, was a bit taller, but quite a bit thinner and held a hide folded into a compact bundle.

Lachish started a deliberately slow walk to his left, heading for the top of the staircase that took the entire side of the courtyard. He methodically took each stair down into the courtyard, holding the rail with a hand loaded with rings. He did most of it for show, aiding the manipulation of negotiation. As he reached the bottom, Abez, the second guard, came in from the entrance.

"Shimon, the weaver, is here to see you, Master."

Lachish took this information in stride. "Show him in." Lachish was pleased to hear this timing and smiled to himself. He knew if there was another watching, he could twist the dealing as the first ones in wouldn't want to act shamefully. He stopped at the bottom of the stairs and waited. Abez ushered Shimon into the courtyard, turned, and stood by Telem.

Shimon saw he wasn't there alone and humbly turned off to the left to stand patiently to the side. Lachish took advantage of the theatrics and walked purposefully until he stood before Uthai. "What have you brought me?"

"This is a sample of what we brought to you from forty such hides." With that, Peretz handed Lachish the folded hide he had been holding. Lachish took it by its edges as if he didn't want to get his hands dirty and let it unfold. He looked down his nose at it as he frowned with a scowl between his eyes.

"This is quite thin. The tanning process will make it even thinner. I need better hides than this. What are you asking for them?"

"A denarius apiece," Uthai offered.

Lachish' face darkened with mock anger. "For this?" He held it up higher, in front of Uthai. "You must want to make me a target for mockery! 'Lachish will pay anything!'" he said sarcastically. "Don't be ridiculous."

"These hides are not thin! A denarius per piece is close to the cost it takes to make and bring them. We need that."

"Maybe you should take them straight to the Tanner. Maybe he will pay you that."

"We tried. He says he won't take any except they come from you."

"Then I suggest you take my price or else you will get nothing for them. I will give you twenty denarii."

"Twenty? I can't feed my family on twenty. At least give me thirty!" Uthai's voice showed desperation. He really needed this to go through. Lachish heard his tone. That was his signal he had won and had the upper hand.

"Twenty-five. That is all I will pay. Or take them to someone else."

"There is no one else!" Uthai reached out and grabbed Lachish by the arm. Lachish glared at him. Immediately Telem leapt in and seized Uthai's upper arm with an iron grip. Uthai looked at Telem, shocked and scared, and instantly released Lachish, pulling his own arm back as if he had touched acid. "Please, I meant no disrespect. I need that money!" His eyes returned to Lachish, pleading, looking for some break in the wall Lachish presented.

Lachish glanced at Shimon, who was watching this all unfold. Acting as if he were doing something highly honorable, Lachish quietly said, "I'll give you twenty-eight for the lot." Then he spoke to Telem, "Pay him and get his mark on the tablet." He dismissed the men with a flick of his wrist, and turned toward Shimon as if they were no longer there.

Uthai and Peretz stood stunned, looking at each other, trying to figure out how they had lost all that money so easily. "But..." Uthai tried to speak more, but Telem used his grip to turn Uthai around and usher him toward the door. The two men stumbled and shuffled forward, finally finding themselves in the guard room. Telem counted out twenty-eight denarii from a leather purse hanging from his belt, then held out a quill and the tablet for them to mark. He stared at them like a rock statue until Uthai reached out and took the quill, hesitantly reaching out and making his mark next to his name. Telem handed him the coins. "Thank you. Peace be with you." With that, Telem stepped back into the gate and closed it, leaving them standing in the street with their mouths gaping.

Lachish moved over to where Shimon stood and bowed condescendingly. "Welcome to my house. I see you have my curtains."

Shimon had just witnessed the vanquishing of the two Jewish men and didn't know how exactly to respond. "Yes, I do. They turned out even better than I had hoped. The dye is exceptionally consistent."

As they were presented to him, Lachish almost tenderly received them. "Oh, they are quite beautiful!" He took the top one, untying the knot in the twine, he released the pressure and let the cloth respond to his touch. As they stood there, Abez picked up the hide from the floor where it had been dropped, refolded it carefully and took it out front. It was as if the other transaction hadn't happened.

The cloth had unfurled, cascading over the floor between the two men. "Exquisite. How much do I owe you?"

"I had told you before that it would cost sixty denarii. That is all I ask."

"Then that is what you shall receive. This is totally worth it. How wonderful they will look in my forward receiving room." Lachish snapped for his house servants who were close and ready. Three young men dressed in simple white tunics appeared, coming quickly to stand in a line just to Lachish' right. One took the rest of the bundles from Shimon while the others retrieved the loose cloth, folding it gently. "Take this up to the steward. They are to be installed today." With obvious nods of obedience, they stepped quickly. "And bring wine!"

With a graceful swing of his hand, Lachish motioned toward one of the doors under the balcony. Shimon knew he was being asked in, but he also knew it wasn't just a request. With a simple bow of reception, he walked toward the door, which seemed to open on its own. As he stepped just inside the door, he was invited to sit on a stool by the door as the servant knelt and pulled close a basin of water. With smooth dexterity, he loosened Shimon's sandals and proceeded to wash his feet and dry them off with a towel that hung on the end of the stool Shimon now occupied.

After wiping down the sandals from the dust on them, he replaced them, tightening the ties expertly. He had done this all without looking up to Shimon's face. He finally stood, bowing slightly, motioning to enter the room. Lachish stood close, taking pride in the efficiency of his staff, whom he had trained. His pride wasn't about them; it was how it made him look that was important.

One of the servants entered with a pitcher and glasses on a tray. In the room, there were several large pillows surrounding a short table in the middle. Lamps burned all around, casting a dim, yellow glow. Easing onto one of the pillows, Shimon deftly removed his *keffiyeh* and stretched out on his left side. The servant poured a glass half full of wine and placed it in front of him. Lachish had walked around him and, gathering up folds of the purple robe, plopped unceremoniously on a pillow close to Shimon's head. The servant moved around them and placed a glass full of wine close to him. Bowls were placed within reach with figs, grapes, and small cakes. The servants then quietly backed up to the walls and tried to merge into them.

"Bring me sixty denarii from Telem," Lachish commanded the servant closest to the door.

"Thank you for paying promptly," Shimon began.

"Why wouldn't I? I value what you've made."

"Well, I was concerned with how you paid those men before me."

The look on Lachish' face changed. His eyes narrowed and his smile turned from culturally pleasant to nearly a smirk. "That was business. They needed to be put in place so they know who is in charge. They are new suppliers to me. I established the way negotiations were to be done. What you made for me is personal. I want what I want and I will surround myself with the pleasures of life. However, I will determine the prices I pay for goods. They will learn. It will be better. You don't like that?"

"I don't mean to offend. I don't want to tell you how to do your business. Those were men of Israel. I feel we have the responsibility to treat men of Israel differently than we treat those who don't know our God."

Lachish just stared at Shimon. He then reached out and took his wine. He emptied it by a third before he placed it back on the table. "I don't need anyone telling me how to live. I will treat anyone in any way I desire. I like my comfort. I like my wine. I like my money. I do fine without doing it 'by the scrolls.'"

Putting a hand to his chest and bowing his head, Shimon said with sincerity, "Please forgive me. Again, it isn't my place to tell you how to do anything. I try to live my life as close to the scrolls as I can, and it always catches me by surprise when differences are exposed. I beg your pardon for my boldness."

"Granted. I didn't want anything to come between us. There are other things I wish for you to make." Shimon saw the arrogance but didn't respond with the sadness he felt. He smiled slightly and bowed his head. The condition of Israel concerned him greatly, but so few were open to the message. Lachish downed another third of his glass, thinking he had won another victory. It was worth celebrating. But, then again, he didn't need much of an excuse to drink.

"Please, try the cakes, they are delicious." Lachish took a couple of the cakes and devoured them, washing them down with a glug from his glass. Opulence served him well.

After eating one of the cakes and having a few sips of the wine, Shimon felt he had satisfied social demands. "Thank you for your hospitality, but I need to continue on my rounds." Lachish closed his eyes and nodded, giving Shimon the permission to leave. Shimon stood, collecting his *keffiyeh*, bowing with his hand on his heart. One of the servants handed Shimon his payment. He nodded to the servant, receiving the pouch. "May the *shalom* of God be on you and your house." Lachish just nodded to him. Shimon turned and strode through the door into the courtyard. He tucked the pouch into his sash, and then placed and adjusted his *keffiyeh* for outdoor travel. As he passed into the guard room, Telem was there with the tablet and quill.

After signing, the gate was opened, and Shimon stepped out on the streets of Jerusalem.

Lazarus was in great pain. He had made it part way to the temple area and felt something snap in his lower leg. His foot wasn't supposed to be at that angle, was it? He sat there on the side of the street, trying to catch his breath. How was he going to beg if he couldn't get to where the people walk by? He saw a couple of men walking his direction. As they got closer, he hoped to be able to get a couple lepta from them. Even if he did, how was he going to be able to get somewhere to buy something to eat? Sweat poured off his head from the pain throbbing in his leg. "Oh, Lord God, help me."

Uthai and Peretz were walking slowly, trying to figure out how they were going to tell the family about not getting enough money. Being swindled by a rich man hurt. Uthai grew angrier as he walked. Even as he walked lost in thought, something broke through to his consciousness. What was that smell? Looking down a little way ahead of him was a beggar.

Lazarus looked at them imploringly. "Alms, please?" He stretched out one hand and supported himself with the other. "Please, sir, I am so hungry."

Uthai stopped just to stare at the man. Peretz looked at Uthai with sadness in his eyes. "What can we do?"

"We don't have anything to give you. We have just been in a deal that took away whatever we would have had."

"Isn't there something you can help me with?"

Uthai looked him over, cringing at the sores and dirt. Lazarus suddenly winced and cried out a little. Peretz pointed to his right foot. "Look. His leg is twisted."

"It just happened. I can't move. Can you help me?"

Taking off his bag, Uthai looked inside, pulling out a small, thin blanket. Taking it out, he started a tear on one edge, ripping a strip from one whole length. He then took the strip and wrapped the foot and ankle, stabilizing it. Every few moments, he wiped his watering eyes from the smell. He tried to breathe through his mouth, hoping it would help him not encounter the odor. Peretz gave Lazarus some gulps of water from his waterskin, Lazarus downing it greedily. Uthai finished, wrapping it with a knot that would hold for a while, then rocked back on his heels as he examined his work. Looking up, he made eye contact with Peretz. Peretz was truly concerned, as was his way. Looking at Peretz, Uthai knew they weren't going to leave this man. Peretz wouldn't let them leave him.

Looking at Peretz, Uthai said, "Come over here. We need to talk for a minute." He stood and walked back up the street a few steps, trying to catch some fresh air. "I have an idea to help this man. Can you stand the smell for a little while longer?" Peretz nodded at him. "Good. Let's take him back to the house of Lachish and set him at the back door of his villa. They will be able to give him food and drink. They have plenty. Does that sound good to you?"

Peretz' face lit up in a smile. That would do it. "They could help better than anything we could do," he replied.

"We'll use the blanket to carry him so we don't have to touch him and his sores. Afterward, he can keep it. What do you say?"

Peretz nodded enthusiastically in agreement. Uthai took several deep breaths to clear his sinuses and went back to Lazarus. "We know a place where you can go. They will be able to feed you and care for you. Is that alright with you?"

That was the best offer Lazarus had had in a long time. "Thank you. That would be wonderful. Jehovah be praised!"

Uthai, putting his bag back over his shoulder, spread the blanket beside Lazarus with Peretz's help. "You will have to try to move over onto the blanket." Lazarus wiggled over, trying not to hurt his ankle. He finally got situated, holding his crutch close to his chest. Uthai knelt behind his head and reached down, putting his arms behind Lazarus's shoulders; grabbing the blanket on both sides of his upper back, touching nothing but blanket and cradling Lazarus's head on his chest. Peretz took the two lower corners, twisted them into handholds, pulled them to the outsides of Lazarus's knees, and started to lift as Uthai pulled him up off the ground. Walking mostly sideways, they proceeded to go back up the hill toward Lachish' villa.

Carrying him required extremely close contact with Lazarus's body being directly under Uthai's nose. It was very difficult to get a full breath.

Consumed in thought, Shimon left the villa with a heavy heart. This was indicative of the condition of Israel. People were too busy trying to gain wealth or accolades to look at their lives before the Lord God. He knew he had to act like a businessman to get the accounts he needed, but how he wished he could do business with people who loved God. He knew men like Lachish who were eaten up by greed, food, and wine. It didn't turn out well for them, but that didn't seem to matter. There was more to life than just living it here, he was sure of it. "We need to open our eyes!" he thought out loud.

Something caught his attention. He looked up to see a strange sight. Two men were carrying a third on a blanket up the hill. He suddenly recognized the two who were doing the carrying as the men who had just been at Lachish's house conducting business and not faring well. As they got closer, the smell hit him. He had known that smell before. When he did his rounds, bringing food and clothing to people, he had run across it. Full of curiosity, he walked toward them.

"Greetings! Do you need some help here?" The younger man was having trouble keeping his grip. Shimon stepped in and grabbed the closest corner, allowing the man to get a better grip with both hands on the other side. "What are you men doing?"

"We are taking this man to the servant's entrance of Lachish's house. They will be able to feed him there," Uthai barely spoke out under the strain of his load. Shimon let the years of moving the shuttle bring in his strength as he helped share the weight. Now they were walking with Peretz and Shimon in front and Uthai bringing up the rear. This was much easier, and they were able to move quicker. As they walked, Shimon had to get used to the stench quickly as he noticed the sores and the wrapped ankle. When he could afford it, he turned to look at the man they were carrying.

"I know you. Aren't you Lazarus? I've given you food before."

Lazarus's face was filled with concern and fatigue. Even though he was being carried, it was hard for him to hold himself in place, and the pain of his foot was getting through to him. "Yes, I know you. You have been kind to me."

When they arrived at the villa, they went down a little alley to the servant's entrance where the business of the household was done. It was a stone enclosure that made room for entering the house and shuffling merchandise. A couple of stray, ragged dogs who had known this place as the source of scraps were startled, ran away a short distance, and then stopped to watch. Turning around with Uthai backing up, they found a place close to the corner, a short distance from the stairs, to lay Lazarus so he would be out of the way but comfortable.

Uthai stepped back, stretching his back from carrying the load. Peretz stood up and shook out his hands from gripping for so long. Shimon rested with his hands on his knees, breathing a little heavy, and asked Lazarus. "Are you alright?"

Sitting up with his back against the wall, Lazarus winced at the pain of his ankle. "I will be much better now."

"Is there anything I can get you?" Shimon asked as he stood up.

"No. You have done so much." Lazarus looked around at the men. "Thank you so much. Your concern has moved me greatly."

Uthai looked at him and said, "You will be safer here. They should be able to bring you something. We need to go, but you should be fine." With that, he motioned to Peretz that they should leave.

"Don't forget your blanket," Lazarus said with humble gratitude.

"Please, you keep it. You need it more than we do." Uthai was glad not to have to touch it again. Peretz only saw it as kindness. He felt good that they had helped this man.

"Can we leave him the waterskin too?" Peretz asked. Uthai knew the heart of his son. He also knew he didn't want to drink from it after Lazarus.

"Most certainly. We can make another one. Blessings on you all. We must leave now."

"Blessings on your way," Shimon said as he smiled graciously at them. The look on Lazarus's face said everything to them. They were off down the street.

"Thank you for doing that, Abba," Peretz said to his father. He felt a lot better than he had after their meeting with Lachish. To him, this made the trip worthwhile. Uthai, on the other hand, looked like he was doing the right thing, but what was in his heart was a lot darker. He had done this to place the horrible smell just outside Lachish' house in an attitude of vengeance. His suffering through the smell was justified with the satisfaction of getting back at Lachish. Both men walked with the step of one who had done something personally rewarding. One of them was correct.

Shimon was concerned for Lazarus, "Will you be alright here? Do you want me to bring you anything?"

"No, please. You have done enough. It is true I should be able to do well from the scraps coming from this big house.

I have seen it before. I will be fine. The Lord God has blessed me this day, and I am grateful."

"Then I will leave you to get rest. May God richly bless you." With that, Shimon bowed to Lazarus and turning also departed.

Lazarus felt truly blessed. He had a place that could give him sustenance, and he now had a blanket and a waterskin. He closed his eyes and recited some Psalms of praise. It almost made up for the pain in his ankle.

Lachish had several more transactions that day. Each one was celebrated with more wine and food. He received reports from his couriers about activities at the warehouse. By evening he was inebriated by it all. He couldn't walk by himself. His wife checked on him periodically, wondering if he was going to be in any condition to join the family for the evening meal. Most days he wasn't, today was no different.

She came to his office after the last customer had left. They had lit the evening lamps and she saw him sprawled behind the low, thin table he used as a desk, propped up by pillows. She came up beside him, kneeled down, and put her arm around his shoulders. He turned his head to her, yet his neck didn't seem to have the strength or control to keep his head steady. Trying to focus on her, he slurred, "What are you doing here?"

"I'm here to help you come upstairs." She held him from behind, nudging him to stand up. Getting him off the pillows was hard and it was a long way up. She had to help him negotiate getting out from behind the desk. His bulk made things more difficult. She couldn't lift him, only encourage him with firm pressure which way to go. She called on a couple of servants to come to help him navigate. He kept muttering about how important he was, and how he had won so many victories today. She kept replying in a low voice, "Yes, you are. I'm sure that is true. You have done well today, but now it is time to come upstairs." All this was a fairly consistent nightly ritual. The wine was clearly in control.

The family lived on the second level, business was conducted downstairs. He liked that the second level had better breezes coming through, keeping it quite cool. His life was one of increasing wealth, but decreasing satisfaction. There wasn't anything enough for him. He needed more food, more wine, more furnishings, more expensive clothing. He lived in comfort in everything but his soul. Now, again, he was being deposited on his bed like a big lump. He had no idea what most people thought of him, be it pity, hate, disgust, or ridicule.

His wife was patient. She took care of him, trying to stay in the background. She tried to give him no cause to focus any of his anger at her or the children. They lived quietly and insulated from him. To him, they were just more things he owned. He had no concern for them and no part in the function of the family. He didn't have to do anything, that was why he paid the servants. His world revolved only around him. It was his only focus.

The next morning, Lachish woke up late and slowly. He didn't remember how he got into his sleeping tunic. He knew his head hurt and his stomach felt queasy. He walked clumsily out from his bedchamber into the family area.

Abigail sat with their children. She was as educated as a woman could be and had taught the children how to read and count. Shemuel had gone to school and was getting close to his bar-mitzvah. He soon would take his place as an apprentice at the warehouse. Lachish could afford to support their family for generations, but it was his plan to have Shemuel take the legacy of the business, like his father.

Peninah was becoming a young woman much faster than Lachish wanted. It wouldn't be long before they would arrange a marriage for her, probably with one of the rich families around them. It would be acceptable to Lachish if she married a Roman. He had no dear ties with Israel, but his children were raised to know the culture and traditions, giving them a future no matter what path they took.

Mid-day meal was being prepared. They were waiting and prepared to eat. Lachish came in and joined them. It was apparent he wasn't feeling well. They were used to that, and knew to give him a quiet berth. He lowered himself onto a cushion carefully; movement was painful. He looked at his son, and something didn't seem right. Shemuel winced almost as badly as he did. Then he noticed they all were scrunching their noses or reacting in some way. As his senses awakened from his stupor, he started noticing something creeping into his awareness. Then he sniffed. "What is that smell?"

Lachish got up, trying to track its source. He started walking toward the kitchen where food preparation was going on. The servants were startled seeing him come in; he never came there. "Where is that smell coming from?" he demanded. The head servant just pointed out the door leading outside. Lachish knew his curiosity might not be a good idea this time, but he couldn't help wanting to know. He went out the door and down the stairs when he finally got a full look at Lazarus laying there. Lazarus was eating a few scraps of food that had been thrown to him. He looked up, and the two men locked eyes.

The sight Lachish saw revolted him. With the pounding of his head and his already nauseous stomach, he wasn't feeling well at all. The open sores were very obvious and the wrapped foot meant the lack of mobility. "Where did you come from?" Lachish now needed to know what was happening just outside his back door.

"Some kind people placed me here to give me some shelter and supply. Thank you, kind Master, for the place and the scraps. I am very grateful." Lazarus knew his predicament was totally dependent on the mercy of the lord of the house.

"You reek! Your stench fills my house! You can't stay here."

"Sir, I am wounded and can't move. Have mercy for a little while until the pain goes down some. I will move on as soon as I can."

"Something has to be done. This is unacceptable."

"I am sorry, my lord, but no one will allow me to come get clean. May I come in and wash?"

"No! Certainly not. I don't want your stench in my house." Lachish was horrified thinking of this creature inside his fabulous dwelling.

"Please, sir. I need something." Lazarus's eyes were pleading with a desperate intensity.

"I will do something, that's for sure!" Looking back up the stairs, Lachish began to yell, "Bring me a bucket of water! Bring it now!" A servant appeared at the top of the stairs with a pail of dirty water from preparing food. He quickly came down the stairs and handed it to Lachish. Lachish turned and threw the water full force on the man below him. The water took Lazarus's breath away, shocking his system. He jerked strongly in reaction to the sudden cold and banged his foot on the hard dirt, causing a spasm of pain to shoot up his leg. The pain made Lazarus pull back violently. He hit his head on the stone wall cracking open a small wound on the back of his head. He pulled his head slowly forward, leaving the blood stain on the wall. His body was chilled, his leg throbbed, and now his head hurt. He put his hand on the back of his head pulling away a bloody palm. As the pain subsided some, he looked up at Lachish who was stunned at the developments.

Lachish didn't know what to do next. He caught some movement at the top of the stairs, and glancing up, he saw Shemuel watching him. Now he felt trapped in what to do. "You can stay there for a while, but I will do something about that smell." Turning to the servant he ordered, "If you smell him, hit him with another bucket of water. I don't want to smell him again. Understand me?" The servant nodded in obedience and fear.

Turning his attention to Lazarus again, all he could do was look at the man. Something about his face captured Lachish's attention. The humility in Lazarus's eyes was a strength Lachish didn't understand. How could he be like that in his condition? There wasn't any bitterness or anger. With everything happening, he was still grateful. It bothered Lachish. Something shook him to his core. He shoved the bucket into the chest of the servant, making him grab it. With another glance at Lazarus and nearly gagging, he mounted the stairs shakily.

The servant looked at Lazarus with an expression of apology, but he knew he was going to have to douse him with water again pretty soon. Lazarus knew it also. He just nodded with a knowing look that released the servant from any culpability. They knew where they stood. The servant left Lazarus to himself.

Alone again, Lazarus surveyed his situation. He was wet. He would dry pretty quickly since it was nearly mid-day. He laid on his new blanket, which was also wet. He pulled it out from underneath him with considerable effort and wriggling. Now it would dry better. He used the corner of the blanket to clean his head wound and wipe his body down some. That may help the smell a little. The bandage on his foot was wet, and the cold water relieved some of his pain. His waterskin had been filled earlier by the servant who found him and had given him some food they were going to throw away anyway. They didn't want to give him good food. For fear of the master of the house, they could only give scraps. All in all, he was better off than he had been for a while, except for the ankle.

The tallying of his situation brought him to praise the Lord God again. "Lord, I am grateful for all you brought me today. Please, help me be wise." All that had just happened had weakened him. He laid down flat on his back and passed into a calm sleep. Sleep felt good. He hadn't had much deep sleep for a while. The pain had kept him awake, but now he slipped into a solid slumber.

He woke up feeling something very strange happening to him. He opened his eyes to see a couple dogs. One of them licked the sores on his leg. It felt good, like it was cleaning it out. The other dog cautiously approached from the other side, starting to lick the sore on his upper arm. For some reason, it felt like they were companions on the same journey. He was thankful for the company. He talked to them in a calm, friendly voice. They soon lost interest and loped on down the road. Lazarus felt the loss of their company. The loneliness crowded in.

As he dried out, the smell started coming back. With the reprieve from the smell for a period, the return affected him. He knew if there was an odor now, there would be a return of the bucket. Mid-afternoon there was a stream of activity as people came bringing supplies for the household. Things were brought in and out. For the most part, he was ignored, but as the stench started returning, the people noticed him more and more. He knew it was only a matter of time.

Closer to sundown, a servant came back out. He had the bucket with him, but he also had a small bundle wrapped in a cloth. He came down the stairs trying not to look Lazarus in the face. He set the bundle aside and, as he was instructed, he threw the contents on Lazarus. Lazarus had tried to keep the blanket dry, but it didn't work very well. The servant picked up the bundle, coming close to Lazarus, he knelt down handing him the bundle as he said softly, "I'm so sorry. I don't have a choice. I hope this makes up for it some."

"Bless you. You are a good man and a good servant. May God bless you and your household." Opening the package, Lazarus found some bread smeared with oil, a small dried fish, and a few figs. His mouth and eyes went wide open with wonder and gratitude. "Thank you so very much! You have blessed me beyond measure today."

The servant stood, retrieved his bucket and with a sad smile climbed the stairs, leaving Lazarus on his own again. He ate his meal feeling like it was a feast. It felt wonderful to have something inside him again. And the taste was grand! With a few drinks from the waterskin, his meal was complete.

The sun was completely down now. Lazarus tried to wrap himself in the blanket as the breeze picked up. He eventually went to sleep, waking up every so often shivering and in pain.

CHAPTER 2
The Beginning of the End

He couldn't get the image out of his head. Lachish could see the beggar's face. There was something different about him. It was as if the beggar owned everything and Lachish owned nothing. His encounter left him with an empty feeling. He was the master, but he wasn't in control. He wanted his son to think well of him, but he knew he had looked bad. What else could he have done? Having him dragged away wasn't an option. He had to do something about that smell, but what? He felt trapped. Nothing he did would have saved the situation. But instead, he felt like the bad person. This beggar seemed to be the one in control. This really bothered him.

There was business to get done, so Lachish immersed himself in it. First things first, though. He ordered wine. Eating lunch was delicious, but empty. He had more food brought. How could someone be so full physically and still feel so empty? The day marched on, but that beggar was still the main thing on his mind. The transactions he was involved with didn't satisfy him today. His mood became more and more sullen. Wine didn't cheer him. It made his body feel flushed and warm, but his soul was chilled and cold. How could someone who had everything be so miserable?

It seemed to be evening too quickly. He went upstairs after dark. Abigail was surprised to see him this early. He actually ate with the family. He walked over close to the kitchen sniffing the air to see if there was any residual odor. He smelled the burning of the oil in the lamps, but nothing out of the ordinary. He caught the servant as he came through on an errand. "Did you do what I told you to?"

"Yes, my lord," he said softly, "It has been taken care of."

"Is he still there?"

"Yes, my lord."

"Keep on it." Lachish had to at least appear to be in control. He went to bed, and even though he had plenty of wine, he slept fitfully.

The next morning Lazarus was awake early. He had finally curled up enough to get somewhat warm. His ankle had calmed down a little. Moving it reminded him what pain was, so moving it wasn't done very often. His head and back really hurt by sleeping on the ground without moving much.

The household had started working. A passing servant coming to work threw him a loaf. Another one replenished his waterskin. He did what he did every morning, starting with some Psalms and recited some of the prophets for good measure. He prayed when the shofar was blown at the Temple. It was another bright day in Israel.

However, something was wrong inside him. He felt differently. He was weaker than normal. He knew it. Sometimes he sweated and then almost immediately shivered. All he really wanted to do was sleep, but even when he could fall asleep it was never deep. He dried out, and when he pulled the blanket off, it had stuck to the sores and reopened them. The oozing had redoubled and with it the smell. About mid-morning, the servant came out with the bucket again. He mouthed to Lazarus, "I'm so sorry." Lazarus just nodded his head and steeled himself for the sensation that was about to bombard his being. After the dousing, Lazarus used the cloth his food had come in the day before to wipe down the sores he could reach. The washing seemed to be helping them, but his core was shaken. The trembling was more consistent.

The business of the day that ushered people in and out of the house was like a machine. It happened around him, but he was losing interest in it. His breathing had become labored with a slight wheezing starting. He had to roll over, wait for a break in the people coming and going for him to urinate toward the corner. He knew he couldn't go anywhere; he hoped this didn't add to the smell. Maybe the dousing would wash some of that away.

He longed for some of the food that was being transported into the house. He wasn't sitting up with his back to the wall anymore. He was laying down with his painful ankle stretched out. He was losing his desire to fight for his life.

The servant came just before sunset. He had the bucket, but instead of throwing it over him, he came and poured it over his legs, letting Lazarus use the cloth to wash his arms and some of his body. Even then, though, the ground was wet. Lazarus shifted over some, but there wasn't much room and the ground was wet just about everywhere. The servant had brought him another package of food and all Lazarus could say was a very quiet, "Thank you so much. Be blessed."

He ate some and stopped. Then he forced himself to eat the rest and drink some water. It felt a little better, but not a lot. He wrapped in his semi-soaked blanket and fell into a strange, comfortable sleep.

Rising earlier than usual, Lachish was exhausted. He didn't sleep deeply, tossing and turning all night. His dreams had been random, unconnected, and disturbing. He stumbled around the house as the servants prepared meals and cleaned. They didn't know what to do with him being up this early. Abigail assured them with a look and watched Lachish wander around. She also didn't know exactly how to respond to him. The only thing in common with most mornings was the wine. He appeared to need some to get himself centered today. Shemuel and Peninah made sure they were as invisible as possible. The household was in an obvious unstable state.

After his day of dousing the beggar yesterday, he was coming unraveled and didn't know why. Why should that bother him? Who was this man? He went to the windows and couldn't quite see him out there, even though he felt his presence. The servants brought in breakfast. The family sat quietly as they ate, everyone glancing at Lachish when they thought they could get away with it.

Abigail tried some small talk, hoping to get him provoked into conversation. "The new window dressing is beautiful. Do you like it?" Lachish broke from his internal musing to look at her, then up to the windows.

"Yes, they look good." With that he looked back down at the wheat cakes he was eating and was lost again in thought. Soon, the silence was palpable. Lachish realized they were all together and were wanting some kind of interaction with him. "I have a full day today. I need to be left alone. I have much business to consider." With that, he dismissed any thought of discussion. Looking up for one of the servants he ordered, "Get Telem. I need to see who is coming today." Now it was understood, all interaction was now over.

Lachish walked out to the courtyard balcony, standing there staring out into nothingness. Telem approached him from the side. Lachish didn't know he had come close. When Telem addressed him, he jumped, shooting a terrified face toward the sound. "Oh, Telem. You startled me. What is on the schedule for the day? Where do I need to be?"

"Today is your day to go to the warehouse and check the books. No one is coming here today at all. What is your desire?"

Lachish was taken off guard, which surprised Telem. Something wasn't right concerning his master. "Very good. Get things prepared to go. We will go when you are ready." Telem bowed and left him standing there. He was trying to get his head together about what the business was for the day but couldn't get his thoughts to obey.

He went back into the house telling Abigail he was going to be gone for the day. As he stood there, the servant he had ordered to douse the beggar came in. Lachish caught his attention, sternly glaring at him he said, "Keep doing what I told you to do yesterday. I want none of his stench in this house. Do you hear me?"

"Yes, my lord." If Lachish had cared to look, he would have noticed the pained expression on the servant's face. Instead, Lachish was only interested in making sure he was in charge. He needed to be in control over something. He wanted to go out and see the beggar, to make him understand his authority. He couldn't bring himself to do it. Knowing the beggar had greater control over the situation rattled him. That stinky man had control over the inner man, much more than Lachish had ever been able to control himself. That fact disturbed Lachish to his bones. His world unraveled before his face.

Telem came out of the kitchen carrying a basket of food and a wineskin. Bowing to Lachish, he said, "Your carriage will be here momentarily. We are ready to go whenever you are." He then moved out to the balcony and down the stairs to his room by the street. Lachish stood for a while, rooted to the floor. His confidence had been shaken. Could anyone else see it? Was he being exposed to those around him? He needed to pull things back in line. Lack of sleep and the wine made his thoughts pull out of reach. He thought that maybe going to the warehouse would clear his mind and help him step away for a few hours. Maybe that would help.

His day was lost in meaningless transactions that would normally have recharged him. Business went on. The books were reviewed, the orders placed, the goods received, the wine drank, the food eaten. Nothing he did felt right.

Finally, the day was completed. Telem helped him mount his carriage, and they were off. He was headed home, but that brought him no comfort. What if that beggar was still there? What was he supposed to do about it? A silent dread filled his heart. He was sweating. He felt sick. Misery was the only thing he had right now. There was no help for what ailed him. He was lost.

Arriving just before sunset, they came from a different direction where they couldn't have seen the beggar, even if he were there. As Lachish got down from the carriage, he looked over toward the corner of the building, knowing that around that corner was the entrance to the back stairs. He didn't go over there, but he did notice a streak of wet ground coming from the back. He knew what caused it. A pang of guilt stabbed him. He didn't like it very much. He wobbled into the front entrance with Telem at his elbow.

Lachish headed for the stairs, Telem helping him. As he reached the stairs, he jerked his arm away from Telem, "I can go up by myself. I don't need you anymore tonight. You are dismissed." Telem simply nodded and bowed.

Lachish stood on the bottom stair with his hand on the rail. With much effort, he made it one step at a time up to the balcony. He was sweating profusely now; breath came with difficulty. He heard the evening shofar blow. It held no significance to him, nothing but an alarm clock to mark the day. He walked slowly into the family quarters.

The evening meal was already being served. He plopped himself down with little grace and with a great grunt. He took off his cap and threw it aside. "Wine!" His thirst was great right then. The day had taken its toll on him. The family stared at him with concern.

"Would you care for some water? Are you alright?" The concern in Abigail's voice was evident.

"No! I called for wine! I'm fine." A servant entered quickly, pouring wine into a glass out of a jar. This was the good wine. He took it and drank a couple of gulps, breathing heavily. He could see the looks on their faces and resented it. He grabbed a loaf of bread, ripping it apart and dipping it in the oil, eating it greedily. He dipped into some of the other sauces and grabbed some fruit. There was prepared meat on a dish and without putting it on a plate, he selected a piece, eating it. He felt awful. He couldn't stand them watching him anymore. He stood with much effort and directed his unsteady steps toward the bedchamber. Stripping off his robes, sash, slippers, and tunic as best as he could, he finally fell on the cushions on the bed and lay there, rasping breath. He was glad to have this day over. He only wanted rest and solitude.

Lazarus awoke not feeling any pain. That startled him somewhat. He hadn't been pain free for as long as he could remember. He wasn't cold. He wasn't stiff. He wasn't even hungry. He looked around, standing up effortlessly. He was still in the little alleyway just off the street, but something felt different. As he looked around, he suddenly noticed somebody laying by his feet. It was a beggar wrapped in a blanket like his. He had an ankle wrapped up just like he had. This whole person seemed familiar. He stooped over to look more closely and was amazed at how clearly he could see, even in the dark. "Is this a dream?" he wondered.

There was something familiar about this man. It was mostly his hands; they looked like he should know them. They looked like the hands he had seen for years. He scanned down the man's form. The feet stuck out from the blanket. The bandage wrap was exactly like his, which made him wonder why he was able to stand up without his ankle hurting him. He looked at his ankle; the bandage was gone. So were the sores. He extended his arms, and all those sores were gone, too. Wait! What was he wearing? Where did that come from? He wore a simple, yet elegant, white, knee-length tunic of extremely fine texture.

He stood there, minutely examining himself. His hands found his face. The beard was full and dark again. It was clean! "If this is me, who is that who looks just like me?" he thought. He had not seen his face in a mirror for many years now. He stooped again, intently gazing into the face of the poor man at his feet. The emaciated face looked a lot like his father. The hair was matted together, and the face was creased and worn. He reached out to touch the face; his hand went right through it without feeling it at all. He jerked his hand back, startled. He tried to move the blanket away for a better view; his hand again went through it. He couldn't move anything or affect it in any way.

Standing erect again, he noticed his feet weren't actually touching the ground. Stepping back in a reaction to what was in front of him, he was several feet back instead of just a step. His mind was racing trying to understand the things that were happening around him. He wasn't able to mentally grasp the things he saw or did.

In his periphery, he noticed movement. Turning quickly toward the movement he saw a being standing a few feet away, being very still, and watching him quietly. He was stunningly beautiful! The man was dressed in white that glowed in the dark street without casting any light on the street itself. He was tall and powerfully built with wavy, long, light brown hair. His hands were clasped casually in front of him. His eyes were gentle, non-threatening, matching the simple smile on his face. "Greetings, Lazarus. Peace to you. Don't be afraid; I am not here to hurt you."

Lazarus stood motionless, completely dumbfounded. "Do I know you?" Lazarus hadn't used his voice until now. It also startled him. The sound was different than he had known it before. It was clear, strong, and confident. A quiet chuckle came from the being in front of him.

"No. I am Dawrak. I have been sent to retrieve you. Your faith in our Lord has affected you. He has sent me to bring you to your place before Him."

"Is that me lying there?"

"That is your body. You no longer need it. It's time is over. You are now free of it. You will have many questions. All will be answered in time." Dawrak put out his hand to welcome Lazarus.

As Lazarus stepped tenuously toward Dawrak, he knew for some reason he could trust this being. "But what about...?" He hand gestured toward the body on the ground.

"All will be taken care of. Your body is no longer your concern. There is so much more for you to know and learn. You will love it, I'm sure." Dawrak beamed broadly. Lazarus put his left hand in Dawrak's right hand in a gesture of acceptance, when a scream resounded just above and behind them. Lazarus didn't hear it or respond to it. Dawrak heard it, looking up briefly but with no concern.

Another spirit appeared, coming out of the upper floor of the house next to them. There, floating above the ground, was a person, extremely obese and covered in filth, with a look of terror on his face. He looked down to see Dawrak and Lazarus bathed in a glow of light. He knew that face. It was the face of the beggar that had plagued his thoughts of late. There beyond them lay the body of the beggar on the ground. Panic was in his eyes as he searched for the reason for the horrible things happening to him. Dawrak ignored him. Lazarus only knew what was in the light around him.

"You will understand more as time goes on. You are safe. You are not alone. You will see more as you are able to grasp it. You are only given to see as much as you can handle. As you get used to things, more will become apparent." Dawrak exuded an atmosphere of calm peace as he spoke. "Ready to go?"

"Where are we going?"

"To a place of rest where you won't have to worry about anything ever again." It was so comforting to hear Dawrak's voice that Lazarus just melted into submission to the process.

With that simple explanation, Dawrak and Lazarus started moving effortlessly, without taking a step or touching the ground. They were floating through the air, but feeling no breeze. They didn't lean forward or use any convention of travel or vehicle, they simply moved.

Lazarus marveled at things passing by. He felt no fear being in Dawrak's presence. "There are many things you don't understand right now," Dawrak said quietly. The sound made it directly to Lazarus without being lost in the travel. They weren't moving fast, Lazarus was able to recognize the various places they were passing. There was very little activity in the streets. They seemed to be heading toward the Temple. "Do not fear. What will happen next will seem strange, but it will all be good."

The smile on Dawrak's face and the peace in his eyes were plenty to calm any fears Lazarus may have had. As they reached the Temple Mount, they slowed slightly, but their direction shifted as they started moving toward the ground. Lazarus was surprised that they didn't land on the ground but continued through it. Even though they went completely underground, Lazarus could still see Dawrak, who still held his hand. Dawrak wasn't looking where they were going, but he kept a consistent face toward Lazarus. The gaze was returned, there wasn't any reason to be upset or concerned. Just as suddenly as they entered the ground, they came into a place of light.

They landed softly. Dawrak let go and looked around. There was no ground, or trees or anything. What they were standing on was soft and firm, but didn't feel like any ground he had ever walked on before. It was as if they were standing in a place made of light.

"Where are we?"

"We are in Sheol. It is the place of the righteous dead. Because of your belief in the Lord God of Israel and your desire to live according to the covenant of your fathers with Him, you are here. You are to receive comfort and peace here. I am just your guide to bring you here. There are others here to lead you further."

Lazarus noticed someone coming toward them. He was a tall, large man with white hair of medium length and a full, long beard. He was walking, not floating, with a steady gait. His robe was white with vertical blue stripes that went over his shoulders. He had an air of authority about him. He walked up to them and said to Dawrak with a welcoming smile, "Who have you brought us this time, Dawrak?

"Abba Abraham, this is Lazarus."

Abraham stepped up and gave Lazarus a warm, full welcoming hug. "Welcome, my friend. You are highly blessed and favored."

Lazarus was overwhelmed. He wasn't used to people coming close to him, let alone hugging him. But even greater than that, was this who he thought it was? "Abraham? The Abraham? Father of all Israel?"

Abraham leaned back still holding Lazarus's shoulders with both hands. "Yes, I am. You will get used to meeting people here you have heard about your whole life." With that Abraham stepped back and turned to Dawrak. "Thank you for your service again. Blessings to you." With that, Dawrak put his hand on his chest and bowed reverently.

"Blessings to you both." Dawrak turned and started floating up and away from them. Soon he was gone as if he had never been there.

Addressing Lazarus again, Abraham motioned and said, "Please sit. Let's talk for a little while." Lazarus became aware of a couple of stones that were there beside them. They seemed to have been there the whole time, but just beyond perception. Abraham sat on one, Lazarus slowly stepped over to the other one, putting his hand out and feeling the stone. It was smooth, cool to the touch, firm, but not as hard as he expected. Remembering how his hand had passed through the blanket just a few minutes ago, he was totally confused.

"It's okay. It will hold you. Things work differently here than what you are used to. You won't ever totally understand it, but you will get used to it. It will eventually feel very natural, but for a while, it will be unusual."

Sitting down felt different. Things didn't feel the same without a physical body. Items still existed, but in a different way, made of different matter. Lazarus could feel the stone underneath him, but there was no pressure on his legs. It wasn't as restful as it used to be, but, again, standing didn't seem to be tiring either. "Dawrak isn't a human. He is an angel sent to minister to people. He was a guide to bring you to the place of rest. Sometimes the angels have to go get people; sometimes they just show up here. None of us know why or what makes the difference. God knows. We say that a lot around here. You are spirit and soul without a body. You will be here until the Lord God determines it is time to go elsewhere. I have been here a very long time. But being here means there is no more time for you. We don't know the perception of time. There is no night or day, just light. We don't sleep, but have total rest. You are here for a reason. The Lord God wanted me here to greet you. I don't know why, but I am glad to do it."

Abraham turned his head quickly to the left, raising his face slightly as if someone were talking to him. Lazarus couldn't hear anything. He noticed Abraham's mouth moving and his hands gesturing as if he were talking to someone, but there was no one there. There was no sound. Every once in a while Abraham would turn to Lazarus as if he were talking about him and referring to him about something. It was very strange, but it was obvious Lazarus wasn't supposed to be in on the conversation. It lasted a few minutes, but momentarily Abraham looked at him with deep compassion. "I'm sorry, my son. I needed to talk to someone and still protect you from that conversation. You have been through so much in your life. Now you are here to be comforted. You don't have to worry about anything anymore."

Abraham stood slowly as if the years weighed heavily upon him. Lazarus rose also, looking at him to see if there was anything he could do for him. "Don't worry, my son. It is not your concern. There is much to show you. Let us be about that wonderful business now. Come. I have people you will want to meet."

Abraham stepped to put an arm around Lazarus's shoulders, turning him in a direction and gently guiding him. They started walking as Abraham directed him, showing him things that were now coming into view.

Lachish woke with a jump. His chest felt like it was on fire. He couldn't breathe. His left arm had pain shooting down it. He was sweating profusely. Panic filled his brain. "What is happening?" he thought as if he could be heard. Abigail lay on the bed beside him, wrapped up in the blanket in a little ball. Lachish rolled off the bed to his left thinking that if he stood up, he might be able to breathe. He took two steps and pain shot up his arm. He jerked his arm close to him to try to stop the pain but it didn't help. He couldn't breathe. He grunted as he tried to cry out. Then it felt like his chest exploded.

Just as quickly, there was no pain. He watched as his body fell forward and hit the ground like a bag of sand. He stood there, looking at himself on the floor. At least it looked like him. He was wearing his night clothing, but he wasn't moving. Everything else in the room looked normal.

Abigail shifted drowsily, looking over her shoulder in Lachish direction. "Are you okay, Lachish?"

He spun to her spitting out, "No! Help me!" She didn't hear him. She just sat there, looking around, trying to see in the dark. "Abigail! I'm right here!" He moved around to stand directly in front of her. She didn't see him. What was wrong with her?

Abigail rolled over to his side of the bed looking for him. She saw something on the floor, and scrambled out of bed to his side, yelling his name. There was no response; not from his body anyway. Lachish yelled the whole time for her to see him. She wasn't talking to him, but to the body on the floor. He realized he was no longer connected to his body and she couldn't see him. He was coming to the understanding he had died. Fear was mounting up like he had never experienced. He was stuck; there was no turning around.

He saw something else exiting his body. It looked mostly human, but extremely emaciated and disgustingly covered in some form of slimy mud. The look in its eyes was desperate hunger. It looked at him with complete understanding, as if it knew everything that was happening. Its presence was somehow familiar but not known. It spoke with a gritty, cracked voice. "You are no longer good for me. You are now one of us. I need to find someone to feed me." With those words, it floated out through the wall toward the city. That was unnerving.

He could see the pile of body on the floor. He happened to look down. He gasped at seeing himself. He was naked, but covered with filth. It was a dark slime that stuck to his arms with strings stretching from his body. It was all over him. It was just like what was on the creepy thing that had just left. The similarity didn't escape him; they were the same. He screamed at seeing it. It revolted him. He reactively jumped back. That reaction propelled him further than he had wanted. He went right through the wall behind him, finding himself hovering above the street outside.

He saw a flash below and to the left. Spinning, he saw an incredible sight. There were a couple of people standing next to a body on the ground. One of them emitted light from every part of him, dressed in a glowing white robe. The other one looked familiar; he knew that face. It was the face that had been haunting him the last couple of days. It was the beggar! What did they call him? Lazarus? Then he looked at the body on the ground. It also was the beggar! The glowing man looked at Lachish briefly and dismissed him. The other one put his hand in the glowing man's hand, and they started moving away.

Lachish knew the same thing that happened to him had happened to the beggar. These men had answers he needed. He had to follow. It was important to him to communicate with them. As quickly as he thought it, he moved in the same direction. His urgency caused him to move faster than those he followed. As he approached them, though, at a certain distance from them, he hit an invisible wall. It seemed to take the power of his motion away, draining his ability to get closer. He could maintain their speed, but couldn't get any closer. He looked ahead and saw many such creatures like the one who had left him before. As the men approached their position, the creatures parted and let them through. The creatures were of every size, shape, and condition, but they all looked human. They were dark, miserable and slimy but didn't try to interfere with the glowing man and the beggar.

As they traveled, Lachish became aware of what he felt. He was hungry. It wasn't like just the hunger he felt after missing lunch, but a deep, insatiable, driven hunger. He wanted severely to consume something. He was on fire with desire. He would have given his entire fortune for some wine. The fiery hunger ate at him. It burned his face, his body, his very being. It was becoming unbearable. So much so, it almost distracted from his purpose of following his quarry. It made it so he needed answers more than ever. He was driven to pursue.

The glowing man and the beggar started to descend toward the ground. Lachish followed. Then they entered the ground! How can I follow them there? With determination born out of desperation, he did just that, sinking into the ground. He could sense their presence and their general direction. At one point he came out to a more cavernous place. He saw them go through a curtain of light, but as he tried to follow, it became as solid as a rock, hurting him as he hit it. He could still see them as they stopped. He saw another man approaching them. "Who is this?" he wondered. Just as quickly, the thought occurred to him that this was Abraham of Old! "How can this be? Maybe there is help there. I am a Jew, a son of Abraham. Maybe he will help me."

He watched as the glowing man departed leaving the beggar with Abraham. They sat down to continue their conversation. "Now is my chance, I may not get another!" Summoning all his strength and reserve, he shouted, "Father Abraham!"

Abraham turned, hearing his shout. He looked surprised. "Father Abraham, have mercy on me! I am tormented in this flame. Please send Lazarus to me so he may dip his finger in water and cool my tongue."

Abraham was fully astonished that one from the other side could communicate with someone in Righteous Sheol. As he watched, he could faintly see Lachish on the other side of the curtain. His face changed as the Spirit of God softly spoke to him. "Have this conversation; it is important for now." His mind was filled with the knowledge of what he needed to know. He was well equipped.

"Child, remember that you fully received your good things in your lifetime, and Lazarus likewise the bad things, but now you are tormented. Besides all of those things being true, it is impossible because a great chasm, a barrier, has been fixed between you and us, so that the ones desiring to pass from here to you are not able, nor can they pass from there to us. This is the way it is for you from now on, and the same is true for us here."

Lachish heard that indictment with great sorrow. As he was ready to start blaming people for not warning him, his mind raced to all the times he was warned about how he lived. Maybe if he thought of others now, there might be redemption.

"Therefore, I ask you, Father, that you send him to my father's house. I have five brothers. If he will witness what will happen here to them so that they won't come here and be tormented in this flame."

These comments were made out of ignorance. Abraham was sure of that. "They have Moses and the Prophets, let them hear them."

"No, Father Abraham," Lachish countered. "But if one should go from the dead to them, they will repent."

Out of deep pity, Abraham answered. "If they will not hear Moses and the Prophets, they will not be persuaded, even if someone would rise from the dead."

Lachish heard these words in complete and utter dread. This meant there was no hope for him or his family. That realization stabbed his heart like a knife. His predicament was final. He hung his head and turned from the scene in front of him. The picture of Lazarus in perfect comfort, knowing he would never experience that comfort again, burned into his thoughts. The inner fire scorched his mind. He started to rise away from the scene he had witnessed. He floated upward coming out of the ground into Jerusalem and a whole new existence.

CHAPTER 3
What Lachish Learns

Lachish knew he had died. How does one process the understanding of life when everything has changed? He knew he had no hope. If this was death, why did he still think? Why did he see the world around him? He had a great need for the familiar, what he had once known. Was that really just a few minutes ago? So much had happened in such a short time. Time? Even time seemed to have changed.

"I need to go home." As the thought came to him, he started moving in that direction. He didn't know how he was moving, that didn't concern him right now. As long as he was moving, that was all that mattered. The hollowness inside him was becoming apparent. He searched for something he didn't understand at the moment, but it was important to him for some reason.

He passed the places he had conducted business for so many years. They held no value to him as he looked at them. They meant nothing to him. Just a few hours ago they were just about everything to him. Was his whole life empty? What was the reason he did what he did? These thoughts were coming to him way too late. Why hadn't he thought about this years ago, when it should have mattered? Everything had been about him; now nothing was about him. Empty. Hollow. Was there nothing of substance in him? The thought made his mind shiver.

His home loomed up in front of him. He floated up a little, adjusting his height off the ground to go into the second floor. It seemed natural for him to float through things.

There was activity happening in there. Abigail knelt beside his body. It hadn't moved any. She didn't have the strength to roll it over. She had yelled for the servants who were just arriving to the room, running in with a look of concern on their faces. They gasped and checked their forward motion for a second, trying to get a grasp on what is going on. Abigail yelled at them to get help. One of them stopped coming in, turned and ran out, heading out into the street and running as fast as they could to the people who were trained in physical problems. The other one squatted down on the other side of Lachish's body, scanning it and Abigail back and forth with no idea what to do.

Hovering a few feet away, Lachish was also yelling, shouting at them to do something and get him back into his body. He tried going around to his feet, flattening out, and floating down into his body. Nothing happened. He tried putting his arms in his arms and his head into his head, but it didn't connect. He couldn't feel anything, couldn't move anything, couldn't do anything. He was totally helpless.

The servant helped Abigail roll him over onto his back. Lachish wasn't prepared for what he saw. The obese body flopped over, making the head wobble back and forth a couple of times, then stopped as it stared blankly at the ceiling. It was the look on the face that disturbed Lachish. It was an expression of horror. It was so strange to see his face like he was another person. The mouth was open a little, frozen into a frowning snarl. The eyes were wide open, staring at what killed him, it seemed. Lachish stared at his face. Why would anyone want to be close to this person? He was revolting and unpleasant.

Then his gaze meandered up to see Abigail. Her expression was almost more chilling than the look on the dead body. She wasn't crying in sorrow over her loss; she was more thoughtful about what was happening to her in her life. As the first servant came in with another man, she watched as he examined the body. He leaned in close to the face, touching the chest. As he raised his head with a very serious demeanor, he shook his head, telling her it was all over. Her husband had truly died.

"Thank you for coming. I thought he was gone, but I needed to let someone else affirm it. What do we do now?" Abigail had no idea. She wasn't connected to the community because of her husband's dealings with the Romans.

"I will send word to the Rabbi. He will make preparations for burial." He was part of the group of people who took care of others in such situations. He also had no idea what to do for Abigail; that was usually in the hands of the women in the synagogue. Since she had no friends, being secluded by Lachish, she had no one to turn to for comfort or support.

"Take his body to his workroom downstairs." The servants gathered a couple more of them, and even the kitchen help who lived close were summoned. It took all of them to pick him up and carry him down the stairs to his room of business. They covered him there with a blanket they found in the room and left, closing the door.

Abigail just sat on the bed staring at the floor. There were no tears, no crying, no mourning. Lachish realized there wasn't any form of relationship there. Her life was now different, but if there was any mourning, she was mourning the fact she needed to do something now instead of letting him supply for them. She was already thinking of what she needed to do to continue living. She didn't love him or their life together. She had become a possession to prove his importance and wealth. Her whole world had just changed.

She went out to the living area where someone had lit a couple of lamps. The servants were standing there, not sure what to do. Everyone was afraid of saying or doing the wrong thing. They had learned this under Lachish, but he was now dead. What was life going to be like now? They were staring at Abigail, looking for some indication of direction or leadership. It became very apparent to her that she was in charge now. "Look, everyone. The master is now dead. There isn't anything we can do right now. Everyone go to bed. Do what you know to do in the morning. We will figure it all out. Good night."

She walked slowly, as if the weight of the world was on her shoulders, back to the bedroom. She lay back down, but sleep wouldn't come easily. Her mind was racing, searching for answers to her world which had become greatly more complicated. One concern was how to tell the children, who had slept through it all, thankfully.

Just before sunrise, she got up and got dressed, preparing for a very long and difficult day. She made it into the kitchen where a couple of the servants were preparing the food for the day. To the youngest, she said, "Go wake Ibneiah. Send him out to fetch Telem." She knew each of the servants by name and history, unlike Lachish who just saw them as objects to do what he wanted. Ibneiah was the very young son of their house servant, whose husband had died. Abigail had taken them in, effectively saving their lives. To Lachish, they were cheap, immediate help.

Lachish had witnessed everything in abject interest. He floated around seeing everything. He had followed his body downstairs, but that soon became disgusting to think about. The body he had fed and comforted was now just a lump of meat starting to spoil. He went back up through the floor to see Abigail talk to the servants. He saw that he didn't really know this woman. She took control. There was more to her than he had ever known. When she dismissed everyone, he floated around the house totally lost as to what to do. He went in and watched his children sleep. He didn't know them, either, except as a commanding, demanding tyrant who lived totally for himself. They had to act perfectly or there would be consequences. His tirades were famous. Right now, though, it was fear that consumed him instead.

He waited for Telem to arrive. He was the only person who really knew Lachish. He was strong, totally obedient, and resilient. Telem had been with Lachish for at least ten years. Now he would hear a friendly voice. Things were stirring up in Lachish and he couldn't control them. He knew them intimately, but now they were there without any constraint it seemed. He could feel the anger rise. Along with it, however, came hunger that was so much greater than a physical hunger. It gnawed at him. His need to consume something for the pleasure of it was palpable. As powerful as those both were, the greatest urge was the need for wine. He had never understood how much he needed it every minute. This consuming set of desires and emotions were almost more than he could stand.

After what seemed like an eternity, Telem came running in with Abez hot on his heels. They ran up the stairs to the family room. There they came before Abigail, who sat in a beautiful chair just outside her bedroom. Telem bowed onto one knee before her with his fist across his chest, and his head bowed low with Abez following suit. "Mistress, I came as fast as I could. What is it I can do for you at this solemn hour?"

Abigail reached out a hand to him, which rather shocked him. "Good Telem. You have served us faithfully for so long. What would we do without you?"

He took her hand, not knowing what else to do with it. His face registered the uniqueness of the situation. "Please, rise. Come, sit. There is much for us to discuss today." He rose and sat on the chair just opposite her. "The master is gone. I don't want his enterprises to fall apart. My family and I need them to continue. You have watched every move he made. You are familiar with every aspect of the business, aren't you? I am elevating you today to be steward of the house of Lachish. I need your help."

Telem's mouth was open as were his eyes in a wide stare at her. "I uhhh . . . I don't know what to say. This just doesn't happen!"

"I know. But this situation is very difficult, and I can't do it on my own. Will you help me?"

Telem dropped back down to one knee with his fist across his chest again. "I am so honored. I will do everything I possibly can for you."

"Then it is settled. We will learn what we need to as we go. I will write a letter to the managers at the warehouse about your new placement. They will need to know quickly how we are to proceed since the master is gone. I will handle all the matters about the house here, but you will have to keep a hand on the business. You must let them know you are in charge and not let them take control from you. I know you, but I don't know them. If we are strong, we will make it out, with the help of our Lord God."

Abigail rose to get pen and parchment. Telem rose to follow her. Abez followed in strict automatic actions.

Lachish, however, was not so compliant. As he heard this, he broke into a flying rage! "No! He is only a servant! How dare you do this without my permission! You will all pay for this insolence!" He struck out at Telem with absolutely no effect. His fist slipped right through as if he weren't there. He scratched at them, trying to beat them. He tried kicking Abigail, his rage in total release. Nothing was touched, nothing affected. He was inept and helpless, which just added to his rage and frustration. His screams went unheeded, unheard. He stayed there trying to strike at everything within reach. His ineffectiveness just made his rage worse. He didn't know how long he spent raging at everything. He finally just stood in the family area crying. His emotions were continuing relentlessly. He didn't get tired. He didn't spend himself on the effort. He could have kept going endlessly.

He finally followed where they had gone. There was a table spread with good food, anticipating the children coming in from bed. Abigail, Telem, and Abez were reclining at the table partaking together! What an outrage! As he approached, he saw his favorite raisin cakes on the table. He instantly desired them beyond belief. He grabbed for one. His hand went through it and the table. He couldn't grasp it. He couldn't pick it up! But he desired it above anything he had ever wanted before. His lust for it was unabated and unrealized. This was his life now, intense desires with no satisfaction.

They had eaten in the time it took for him to try to satisfy his desires. They rose. Abigail said, "I will get the letter to you, but right now I have to attend to the children. They still don't know." She headed toward the back rooms, leaving Telem and Abez there. The two of them decided to go down to the guard room to work on the things they needed to do.

Lachish followed Abigail. She went into Shemuel's room. He was just sitting up, stretching and rubbing the sleep from his eyes as she entered. She went over to his bed and sat down next to him, giving him a good hug that lasted longer than normal. Shemuel wondered what was up with her. She released him and moved back to arm's length, holding both shoulders in her hands. With her head leaning slightly forward, she looked him in the eyes, capturing his attention.

"There is no way to tell you this easily. Your father died in the night. He is no longer with us." Shemuel's face furrowed into a look of concern. His mind ran through the information, trying to get a handle on it. "But don't worry. We will be fine. I have started taking care of things; you are completely safe."

"Father is gone?"

"Yes, he is. You have nothing to worry about." With that, she pulled him in for another hug. He responded with putting his arms around her and holding the hug for a good long time. Shemuel didn't cry. The look on his face was almost relief. "So, get dressed. We have much to do today and you will need to be ready."

Lachish was stunned. Even his son wasn't grieved at his passing. He again was enraged, but instead of trying to strike anything, he just screamed at them. "Ungrateful whelp! You are useless! I was building you an empire!" Lachish had no ability to see that all Shemuel had wanted was a relationship, not a business. Again, he had missed the important things. He was feeling even hollower.

Abigail moved to Peninah's room. She could sleep until midday if allowed. Abigail leaned over the form in the bed, gently stroking her hair from her face. "Peninah. Time to get up. It is a very big day today and you need to get up and get ready." Peninah woke slowly, trying to make sense of her world, squinting through eyelids that were stuck shut with sleep. Blinking, she finally looked out from the tiny slits, hoping very little light would get in. She couldn't speak yet, just grunted a little to acknowledge her mother had gotten through. She would be a loose bag of bones for another half an hour, no sense in telling her anything for a while. "Get dressed and ready, and then come find me. Okay?" The grunt that emanated from the little, seated pile of person was sufficient communication for Abigail. She got up and left the room.

For some reason, it was important to Lachish to interact with this little lump, but nothing he did got any response. He didn't know her. He didn't know her personality. She was so cute with her saggy, slumber-induced face. The hollowness again ate at him. He would never know her. She was lost to him. He was now meaningless to her for the rest of her life. The sorrow and frustration hit him like a fist. He couldn't handle seeing her any longer and floated out of the room.

Lachish aimlessly floated out to the courtyard. He heard Telem and Abez in the guard room in animated discussion. They had never been allowed to make this much noise. He went there to see why.

"Can you believe what just happened? I haven't expected anything to change for a very long time. The mistress actually believes in me! I can now think of having a future." Telem expressed joy that had never shown in him before. In fact, he had never shown any emotions before. He had always been a stoic, stable presence Lachish could count on. No matter what happened, he could trust Telem to be the same and deal with things. "That fat idiot isn't running things anymore. How he made all that money is beyond me. I don't know anyone who liked him or even enjoyed being with him. I had to put up with all the stupid things he did and make him look good. You know how many times I had to smooth things over with the merchants he dealt with?"

Abez sat there grinning, nodding his head in total agreement. This newfound freedom just might be the answer to their lives. More involvement meant more money. It was a party atmosphere in the guard room. It sure didn't feel like someone had died.

"Well, my friend, I will take care of you as I get things solid. It will be good to be able to do more for my wife and children and feel like I can go somewhere now."

Wife and children!? Lachish was mortified with what he heard. He had no idea Telem was married, let alone had children. But it was the disrespect that slapped him. He thought he ran his world with a tight fist. Now he was hearing that his bodyguard was making his business work; and had been for a long time. He had been reduced to a meaningless clown that was the mockery of the supply chain for the Roman empire. Was everything about his life a lie? Did everybody hate him? Was anything worthwhile? It was too much for him to hear all this right now. He needed a glass of wine.

No one in the household was drinking. It was only he who drank. He knew where the wine vats were. He instantly found himself in front of them in the back cellar. He couldn't get any wine out of them. He even tried to stick his head in the vat itself. Instead of drowning or getting a drink, he got nothing out of it. His entire being screamed for wine. There was no satisfaction here.

Nothing here was good for him. Everywhere he turned he was reminded how badly everyone thought of him. He received no solace. His death seemed to benefit everyone. They were much better off without him. The lie of his importance choked him. He had worshiped himself and discovered too late that he wasn't worth worshiping. With great sorrow, he slowly moved out into the street.

Disconnected. Lachish had nothing that connected him. Family. Business. Social standing. Nothing. Everything had been stripped away. No, it had been torn out from inside him. He was hollow, except for the burning desires that raged within him. The yearning inside him was fierce. He craved pleasure and release. Where was he going? He didn't know, but he was moving. It was like something was calling for him, he gravitated toward something.

It was still early morning. People were just starting to move out into the streets for the day's activities. There were too many people, he noticed. He saw throngs of people everywhere! Was there a festival he didn't know about? That mystery barely registered, but it did surprise him a little. He seemed to be going to the more disreputable places of Jerusalem, the seedier side of the city. He saw a wine den with people milling about. "Why here?" he wondered. It felt like he should be here, he was being drawn inside. He went through the door without opening it.

The place was dark and closed in. There were some people inside in various states. The wine merchant was busy cleaning up, making things ready for the day. There were a few men sitting around with their bowls of wine already. Some were in the corners sleeping off the night of drinking. It was the others that caught his attention. A lot of people were very interested in the men who were drinking. It was then he noticed the difference. The men who were drinking were completely unaware of all the people around them. The onlookers were staring at them, anxiously waiting, watching. The drinkers had a thin layer of light around them as if it were attached to their skin. It moved as they did. The bystanders didn't have that glow, faint as it was. Instead, they had the look of desperate hunger. They would snatch at the bowls of wine without affecting them at all. They would try to drink out of them and get nothing. The effort frustrated them even more, causing them to rant and scream. They were all emaciated and drawn, covered with vile filth. The sight was deeply disconcerting.

Lachish noticed he couldn't take his eyes off of the wine. He was intensely aware of its presence. Oh, how he wanted the wine. It was extremely important to get some. He had a common bond with it. He didn't understand how he could be attached to it, not just attracted to it. He saw the others without the light how they were also drawn to it, also. The whole room had this same feeling in common. They were worshiping at the altar of wine. They were trapped.

One of the drinkers covered in the light was drunk to the extreme. He wobbled like he was losing his ability to hold himself together. Finally, his eyes rolled back into his head, his slack-jawed expression went limp, and his head slipped past the point of control and down he fell. At that exact moment, his glow split at the top and opened a bit. Two or three of the non-glowing people jumped into the man through the crack. Lachish was dumbstruck. He obviously didn't understand what had just happened.

A man standing between him and the passed out drunk got very upset, ranting and raving, using every form of expletive available. He turned around in his rage right into Lachish's face. "He was mine! Mine! I wanted him, he didn't belong to those others!" He lashed out with blinding speed, trying to hit Lachish with his fist. Lachish instinctively tried to block it, but nothing happened. The blow went right through him without hitting him and without any pain. After a second and another attempt at punching him, the man just stood there eye-to-eye with Lachish. It took a moment or two before the man's demeanor changed a little as he examined Lachish. "Ah," he said, "you are newly dead."

"Yes, I am. Just last night. All of this is new to me. I don't understand what is happening." The plea in Lachish's voice was unmistakable.

"You will understand it all by and by. You aren't going anywhere for a long time. Most will ignore newly dead; it doesn't matter to us what happens to you. However, I like telling others about their newfound situation and watch the hope drain away so you are as miserable as I am. You are dead! Dead! There is no hope for you anymore. The only ones who have hope are those who believed in Yahveh and His Messiah. You and all these countless wretches and I are doomed. We worshiped ourselves and what we wanted. We did whatever we wanted and hurt everyone we knew. We got ourselves tied into wine, or food, or fornication, or murder, or whatever our lives focused on." He gestured wildly, spitting every word like it tasted badly.

"We dead are tied to what we desired in life. We tuned ourselves to want it. Now we want it more than ever without the possibility of actually feeling it. The only way we can get close is if there is an opening for us in one who is still alive. They are covered with their life force so we can't get into them. But once in a while, they come so close to dying without actually doing so, that their force opens for a second and we can get in. For a time we can feel what their soul is feeling. We can't feel the body, but we can feel something of the soul, and that is close enough for a while. When we are in there we can drive them to want it even more so we can feel something. It lasts differently in different people, but it lasts for a bit."

He seemed to be winding down a little. "We never sleep. There is no reprieve. No rest. The live ones sleep. They rest. All we can do is wait and watch." The sadness in his eyes was pitiable, if Lachish had had any emotions of that sort to spend on him. "You will find out where you can go and where you can't. Sometimes you can link up with others and it helps somewhat, but it doesn't last for long. If only we had listened to God."

Lachish was horrified. This was his existence now? How could it have come to this? The words of Abraham came back to him. "You have Moses and the Prophets." Ignore those and everything was destroyed in your life.

"I am Beor. I have been around for a long time. I have no idea how long, time doesn't pass well for us. My sons are here, my grandsons. My legacy is not a good one. We all just burn." His voice trailed off as he examined his life and choices. He simply wandered away, consumed in thought and self-pity.

Shaken to the core, Lachish stood there watching everything around him, trying to absorb the information he had just been given. He could see the sad, condemned spirits bent on trying despairingly to satisfy empty desires. His whole soul shuddered at the contemplation. Misery was now his lot in this afterlife. He had no idea it was going to get worse. He just knew he had to strive to bring answers to his longing. He became part of the throng of hopeless beings.

CHAPTER 4
Shimon's Calling
3 B.C.

"I just want to die." Shimon walked slowly toward the Temple. He had been going this route for many years. He had been going to the Temple to pray every day but the Sabbath for more years than he cared to count. His halting gait made the trip much longer, it seemed. The Temple was drastically uphill from his home, and every year it seemed steeper than the last.

He was old. Very old compared to others around him. He had been living in Jerusalem for just over eight decades. He felt very fortunate to be able to walk and go wherever he wanted, but these days it was getting more and more difficult. He increasingly relied on his walking stick. The problem was that because his hands hurt from working so many years, gripping the stick was painful. Every knuckle was pronounced, but the strength they had was still visible. Now, it took longer just to stand up from a stool. He worked at his posture, not wanting to become bent over like so many he knew. Stand straight! Pull back those shoulders! Raise up your head like you are proud to be part of Israel. With that inner rebuke, he straightened his body to its full height. He was taller than most with a thin, wiry body. He continually reminded himself not to succumb to the gravity of the years. He had told so many people that they should present themselves as those who were in covenant with the Lord God of Israel, with a certain pride they were chosen, while still being humble before God.

But today it seemed as if gravity had increased. Even his *keffiyeh* weighed heavy on his head, even though he had worn this traditional headscarf and band to hold it on, his entire life. It was trying to push his head into his shoulders as if to make him bow to the inevitable. Today's walk was almost grueling work. His sweat crept out from underneath his *keffiyeh* and ran down his wrinkled face only to be sopped up by his grand expanse of long, white beard.

The sun beat down on him mercilessly. There wasn't even a hint of a breeze today. It was hot, stifling. It was only mid-morning. What made it worse was the dust. It was kicked up by the hundreds of people in the street today, going about their business for the day. Street vendors with their goods on display, hawking their products to everyone who ventured by. People were busy about their business, each one ignoring the others as if they were totally alone, but intermingling in a crazy dance, whirling about each other in an intricate parade. They intertwined inexplicably. He nearly didn't notice them. He moved so slowly the people had to move around him. His course was staid and clear.

He wiped the dust and sweat away from his eyes with his sleeve. The physical things he was dealing with were a constant drain, but not as much as the emotional, spiritual pressure of his thoughts. He had been an elder in the community for a long time. Before that he was involved in the synagogue, very vocal in the meetings, understood as one who passionately knew the scripture with a deep love for the things of the Lord God of Israel. He had studied, taught, argued, and sought out how they were to live in expectation of the coming of the Messiah. People no longer lived as if something were to happen. They lived their shallow lives, living as if this was all there was or would be. They would do their obligatory services at the temple, go to synagogue meetings, limit their movement on the Sabbath, but live as if there were no God the rest of the time. The coming of the Romans didn't help.

The occupancy of the Romans in the city was ever present. One was always reminded they were the governing power and had been for sixty years. From heavy taxes to oppressive laws, every day was under their heel. Putting an Idumean over them as a symbolic king was an insult. Herod was a thorn in the hand of Rome used to goad the people of Israel. At least he had worked on rebuilding the Temple, but that project was on its seventeenth year. The men of Israel were more politically angry than spiritually motivated. It weighed heavily on Shimon's heart. That was all the men wanted to talk about. "The Romans this... The Romans that... We are oppressed and need our freedom." Even the coming of the Messiah was viewed as a political hope, not a spiritual one. "He will set up His Throne in Jerusalem and overthrow the hand of the Romans!" Couldn't they see the Messiah as the one to come to bring spiritual freedom? There was so much more at stake than governmental power. Shimon bowed under the heaviness of all this. He was getting tired, very tired. He prayed. He talked. Very few listened. It got through to him. He was getting deeply discouraged and had been for some time now.

"Lord God of Israel. I have lived a long time. Everything has been the same for so long. When is there going to be a visitation? We desperately need You to touch your people Israel." The despair of his heart's cry weighed heavily on his heart. The heat and the exertion added to his emotional burden. He stopped for a rest, sitting down on a small stool placed in front of a simple house. There was some shade here. He knew the people who lived here wouldn't mind him using their stool for a few minutes.

The heart burden wasn't alleviated by the break. He leaned forward using his walking staff to prop himself up as his head bowed in deep prayer. He uttered the words the Psalmist penned so long ago, "How long, O Lord?"

For some reason, the street suddenly wasn't busy. A gentle breeze fluttered by, cooling his sweaty brow. The moment was peaceful. He was alone in the rare quiet as his cry issued forth out of his inner being.

A very tender reply came to his attention. His heart swelled up as he heard deep within him, "I have a purpose for you. You will not die until you have seen the Lord's Messiah." The words exploded inside him as a euphoria filled him with delight. His whole life felt fulfilled as he sat there, overwhelmed by the presence of the Almighty God. The years of tedium and drudgery were melted away as he realized that everything had been done to bring him to this place at this time for the reason that only Heaven knew. Now he could see how the steps of his life were ordered to bring about some higher purpose he had never been able to see before.

Something had changed. He didn't feel tired and worn out. He had a role to fill, a purpose for living. Tears came to his eyes as he let praise rise to express the joy he felt. He had no idea how long he had been sitting there. It suddenly occurred to him that people were walking by on the street. It was noisy like normal. It was still hot, but he didn't care. There was something to look forward to, not just life dragging on.

Shimon had been telling people for years that Israel was to be comforted by God. It had taken so long he had started to doubt his own message. Now there was new hope springing up, overwhelming the drain of time that had started to take a toll on him. He didn't regret any of the time spent praying, reading the scrolls, talking with the other elders, or attending the synagogue. It all was a part of what God was doing within him, preparing him for service. He was going to see the Lord's Messiah! It didn't matter now if he lived another eighty years.

She sensed something happening but couldn't put her finger on it. She was old to the extreme, but every day she woke up with one purpose on her mind. She was going to go to the temple and pray.

Hannah had developed a sensitivity over the years to what was real and what was just religion. She lived very close to the temple; it was the only place where she felt at home. She spoke to everyone she could about how God was the one and only God. She told them there would be a redemption for Israel. She knew they needed to live better lives. The people had become complacent. They had lived in the shadow of the Temple, but life had become routine. Religion became something they did, but it didn't truly affect their lives. They showed an outward form of godliness but denied the power within it. She lived by example to those who would see. Some people were still seeking the Lord Jehovah; not many, but some.

Of all that came to the Temple, the one she always enjoyed seeing was Shimon. He was old, but not as old as she was. Shimon had never known her husband. She knew him as the child growing up that had retained an interest in the things of God. She saw him get married and raise sons to be godly. Hannah had liked Shimon's wife, Rebekah. It was a great heartache to see her die in childbirth of their second child. She knew the strain it placed on Shimon. She saw him marry Joanna, whose husband had died, as a mutually advantageous arrangement, but life was hard for them. She had died several years ago, and Shimon had moved in with his eldest son. Life had simplified for him. Now he was able to concentrate on what he felt the Lord had for him in this life. Shimon had never forsaken the Temple or the studying of the Torah and the Prophets. Hannah highly respected him for that.

She was poor. She was, however, a widow in Israel. It was good politically and socially to be seen helping a widow, so she had several who took it upon themselves to help her regularly. It made life so she could spend the time in prayer. She had a small room and consistent food. She had simple needs which were met sufficiently.

She had married young, but how she had loved her Caleb, the young man with the glint of mischievousness in his eye. His ready smile and quick wit lit up every room he entered. The future looked very bright for Caleb and Hannah. Then came the day of tragedy when a wall fell over catching Caleb under it. He died quickly, but she was left alone. She was devastated, and grief overtook her. In despair of life, she became a target of pity. No one wanted to marry her. Caleb had no brothers to raise up children for him so that avenue was not extended to her. She allowed her grief to become her life. After a few years living like that, it appeared she would waste away and die.

One day, as they were reading the psalms in the public readings at the synagogue, she was struck by their message. It seemed as if they were talking to her. The hope was astounding. She could feel the despair David felt as he wrote. But it didn't end there. She felt his hope as he put his trust in the Lord God Almighty. She experienced the peace as it washed over her. She learned the reason she existed. She was to love the Lord God. From that day forward, she devoted herself to learning and prayer. Every time there was a reading of the scrolls, she was there listening intently. Being a woman, she wasn't allowed to read the scrolls herself, but she would be there when others would read them. Her friend Shimon would read for her. Now she not only knew the Psalms but the Torah and the Prophets as well. She loved the prophets. Hearing about the Messiah thrilled her. That was her life's focus now.

It had been eighty-four years since her beloved Caleb left. She understood the purpose of her life would not have been fulfilled in the normal way of living. She might have missed the plan of God for the planet had Caleb lived. There would have been other joys, but what she had now was far greater for the higher understanding.

Now her everyday routine was out of necessity. Every move had to have a reason and be thought out precisely. Every step had to be done on purpose. Her cane was an old hardwood stick with a knob on the top that her gnarled hand fit over perfectly. Her stick wasn't very long since she was a small woman to begin with, and was now even shorter after being bent over with age.

Her face was an assortment of crags and crevices. Her nose seemed to take over her face and was the first thing that came into a room by a good distance. Her hair had grown coarse, hard to deal with. Because she was so bent, her hair was always in her face, so she tied it tightly behind her head as best as she could. It wasn't always well controlled or symmetrical. Her headscarf covered it, mostly. It didn't cover her eyes, however. Her eyes were still bright, ignited by a fire behind them. The body might be crumbling, but the mind was aware and thoughtful. Her meditations and prayers had kept her intelligence intact and fully functional.

Her breakfast was mostly an oatmeal mash. Her teeth had abandoned her years before. It was hard to chew anything, so everything had to be soft and easy to swallow. The preparation was exactly routine so she could get it all done. It was laboriously slow, but eventually, she was ready for the day.

She heavily used her cane as she hobbled to the Temple while it was still dark. She was always there at the lighting of the Menorah. She was there that day last year when the priest named Zacharias had an angelic visitation that had struck him unable to speak. It was remarkable when his wife, who had been barren their whole lives together, became pregnant and gave birth. It was just as remarkable that he regained his voice just in time to name the child John. What a scandal! No one in either family was named John. They had said that the angel had told them to name him that. Was this the beginning of God doing supernatural things in Israel again? She made sure not to miss another visitation like that! Hannah was sure something was in the air.

Now she stayed in the Temple Court-of-Women all day, watching people and talking to whoever would listen to her. She had built quite a band of plain folks who wanted the same thing she did. They would bring her bits of food throughout the day. She had a spot on a stool on the south wall of the Court-of-Women where it was out of the sun and cooler. She was fairly close to the treasury receptacles, and some people would give her a little offering to keep her body and soul together as they came to give their tithes and offerings. She was well established as a fixture of the Temple and people actually expected her to be there day by day. Her friends would find her leaned back against the wall snoozing several times a day.

She spotted Shimon coming in and noticed a new life in his step. What had happened to him? Shimon was more distracted but peaceful. He looked up, seeing her almost immediately. He made eye contact with her. The look on his face was something she hadn't seen in him in years. There was a joy coming out of him that affected her in a beautiful way.

"Hello, Hannah. How are you today?"

"That isn't the issue. What has happened to you?"

"What? What are you talking about?"

"There is new life in you. Something happened. What is it?"

Shimon's face lit up. He lowered his gaze as if he were embarrassed over something. "Oh, you noticed."

"How could I help it? You are glowing! You aren't the same man I saw yesterday."

"It is hard to explain. But if there is anyone who would understand, I suppose it would be you." He looked at her, trying to find the words to describe the indescribable. "I have heard from the Lord." He looked through her as if he were looking into another realm. His eyes shone with a playful gleam as he recounted his experience of the morning. "I heard Him tell me I wouldn't die until I saw His Messiah." He barely spoke over a whisper as he considered what was said so sacred. "I have a purpose to do. I have a part to play in this life as God's hand is working in Israel again." There was no bragging in what he said; only a celebration of the magnitude of this development.

His words sank into Hannah's understanding slowly and steadily. Her eyes grew wider as the realization developed. "He is close."

Neither of them registered the hundreds of people around them as they stared at each other in the revelation of the moment. They were, of all people, most blessed. How could anything be better?

Shimon finally broke the connection. "I will have to meditate on this. I need to be alone for a while. I will be back tomorrow. God bless you mightily." With that, he bowed slightly, touching his hand to his heart in an honoring gesture, and parted with a smile that told her he was in the hands of God.

She watched him leave, marveling on what had transpired. Could it be true? Of course, it was. The culmination of the ages was on the verge of manifesting right before their eyes. How did one comprehend all of this? She would just have to trust her God to bring it all together. She sat and waited for the evening sacrifice, pondering the beauty of the day's events. She would go back to her little room across from the Temple where a simple meal and her bed awaited her. Her life had become beautiful once again.

Shimon went straight home. The way was easier going home, not just because it was downhill, but his mind was filled with so many thoughts that he was distracted. It seemed but a moment, and he was home. He could hear the activity in the rooms beside the house. His first born, Baruch, was busy at the loom making cloth. He had learned this from Shimon at an early age, and they had worked together for many years. Baruch had taken over as Shimon had grown too old to work the shuttlecock efficiently. Shimon had brought him in to learn just after his bar mitzvah. His boys had worked there, building quite a business over the years. Chaim didn't have the fortitude to run the business, but Baruch was a natural. Chaim was less practical than his older brother. He would work well, diligently staying on task day after day, but he was content to work and go home. Shimon had named him "Life" to combat the stigma of his mother dying to give birth to him.

Both boys concentrated on their work. Shimon didn't want to disturb them; he had other things on his mind. The shop was an organized chaos with all the employees busy doing all the parts of the complex world of weaving. He went into the house. Susannah was working hard preparing a mid-day meal for the workers in the shop. Her long dark brown hair framed her face so beautifully. As she looked up and recognized Shimon, her ever-ready smile broke forth in full glory. She was average in height and build, mostly unremarkable until you got to know her. Her excellent beauty came from within her. She had known Baruch all of her life. It was understood at an early age they were going to be together for life. Her bride-price was a joy to pay, sealing the deal for their betrothal. The wedding was spectacular, celebrated by all their close friends. Now she ran the home so Baruch could concentrate on the business. Their children were a blessing and they didn't get away with much under her scrutiny.

She was excellent at managing the household. At times she worked at the spindle making thread for the looms. She was a dream as a daughter-in-law and loved Shimon. She looked up from the bowl she stirred, genuinely happy to see him. It was unusual to see him this early in the day. "Are you going to join us today for the mid-day meal?"

"No, I'm not hungry right now. I will join you later. You go ahead and be blessed." There was a peace about him. He felt it deeply. He knew it showed on his face but didn't want to talk about it to anyone right now. All he wanted was to stay in the presence he had been feeling since his encounter this morning. He quietly stepped through the house and out into the small courtyard. It was peaceful out there. Everyone gained access to their rooms through this courtyard. There was lived-in chaos out here. They kept stores of dry grain and goods in the corner, with capped jars of oil and water. They had made a textile canopy that was spread over most of the courtyard to protect them from the scorching sun. He went over to the sturdy bench placed by the wall of the house. After leaning his walking staff beside the bench, he sat and put his shoulders and head back against the wall. He wanted to just sit in the shade and contemplate life in Jerusalem. The noise and bustle from the street was a distant hum he ignored completely.

He removed his *keffiyeh*, placing it beside him on the bench. He liked to think without anything on his head when it was hot like today. The breeze started, it felt good. He closed his eyes, letting his mind drift to the Psalms he had learned when he was but a child. "Bless the Lord, O my soul; let all that is within me bless His holy name!" Exaltation and praise lifted his spirit as he ran through the entire psalm, each piece building a crescendo of worship. He sensed a closeness to the Lord he had never felt before. His reason for living had been brought to a complete and focused whole. He was part of the plan for the universe, and it greatly fulfilled him. He felt nothing but praise to the Lord God Almighty for this grand opportunity. "Oh, Lord my God. Make me a useful vessel for your purpose. May I hear you clearly. May my heart submit to your every desire. May I be used by you in any way you see fit. You are exalted, oh Lord."

Time didn't register to him. He finally was aroused from his meditation by activity coming through the house as the family had stopped working and was coming in for the end of the day. The sun had begun to set. Shimon became aware of how thirsty he had become. It seemed as if he hadn't moved a muscle all afternoon and now he was stiff and needed to move. Standing up was painful. It took a while for his body to respond to the command to walk. Even though he was still old physically, there was new life in his soul. He was seeing things differently now.

As he entered the family room, he saw the normal life he had seen every day, but today was different. There was a reason this family existed. Shimon could see there wasn't just normal drudgery, but life! His youngest grandson was the first to acknowledge his presence. "S'ba! Sit with me!" Elihu was eight years old. He had a zest for life; everything was wonderful to him. He was a force to be reckoned with, trying to keep him settled and focused.

The table was low to the ground with pillows all around it. There was a place next to Elihu with a cup of wine and a bowl of soup in front of it. Shimon slowly and painfully crouched down, finally plopping heavily onto the pillow, letting out a low groan. He took a deep breath and positioned himself on his left side within reach of the food being passed. Rustling Elihu's hair, he spoke with a hint of mischief in his voice, "What have you been up to today?"

Elihu fixed his gaze on Shimon. Their bond was unmistakable. "I caught three lizards today! We made a cage for them and took them to Micah's house. His mother made us let them go. One of them lost a tail, and we still have it. Want to see it?"

"Maybe later. We need to eat now." What a difference he felt. Had he let himself get so negative in his thoughts that he had been missing out on the joys of living? Feeling he had a purpose again made everything come alive. Shimon used the cloth sitting on the table for him to cover his head. The family waited for the eldest to bless the food. He spoke the blessing he had spoken for many years. It amazed him that it sounded different. It wasn't just words, but deep meaning to him. "Blessed are you, O Lord of the Universe, who gives us bread to eat." He meant what he said. It stirred his soul. The food took on a new value. Amazing what an encounter with the God of Israel will do for your outlook on simple life.

The business of eating went into full effect. Food was being passed around. Elihu didn't miss anything, filling his plate and emptying it with relish. What a wonder to see Elihu in all his celebration of life in the here and now. He watched as the family interacted and ate with such pleasure. He was quiet as he just ate and listened, totally satisfied taking in the happenings.

Baruch noticed the change. "Are you okay, S'ba?" When the kids were born, Shimon had graduated from Abba to S'ba. It was an honor he carried gladly. Shimon looked over to his son, being brought back to participating instead of just watching.

"I'm quite well, my Son. Quite well." He knew he couldn't tell anyone about what happened since it was so hard to explain. This was for him to carry and process.

"Just checking on you," Baruch said. "I haven't seen you all day, and you looked refreshed. It was a good day for you?"

"Remarkable. It was a very uplifting day for me. It is good to see you all doing so well." There were smiles all around. This was a great evening of family closeness. It did his heart good.

As dinner wrapped up and the lamps were making the room smoky, stinging the eyes a bit, the conversation lagged. The children were getting sleepy, and the parents were winding down. Shimon felt his age, experiencing a good kind of fatigue he hadn't known in a while. It was time for bed.

He tried to get up slowly; he just didn't bend like he used to. Elihu and Uriah both moved to help him since they were closest to where he reclined. He needed their help; it was appreciated. He acclimated his body to standing after reclining for a while before he tried walking. Elihu had to show him his lizard tail trophy with much fervor and storytelling before his mother started pushing him toward his room. "See you in the morning, S'ba!"

"You be blessed with good sleep, Elihu." He greeted each one as they left or stayed to talk or clear the table. Shimon walked toward the courtyard with slow, small steps. He picked up his *keffiyeh* he had left on the bench and headed to his room. His was on the ground floor since the stairs were tough to handle. He entered with a lamp he had taken from the family room, placing it on the stand lighting up the room with a dim, dull, flickering glow. His bed mat lying on the sturdy frame in the corner invited him to rest. He removed his sandals and untying the sash of his robe, he undressed, folding it all into a neat, compact pile. He put on his sleeping tunic, blew out the lamp and lowered himself onto his mat. Easing back in the dark, he placed his old, tired head onto the roll he used under his neck. He pulled the blanket up, stretching it out and set it beside him. He might not need it tonight, but there it was, just in case.

He sighed deeply as he readied himself to sleep. His mind went over what had happened earlier. The effect it had was for him to turn to his God. He praised God, reciting one Psalm after another, thanking Him for the extremely wonderful day. He drifted off to sleep in a euphoric cloud of thoughts.

CHAPTER 5
Prophecy

Shimon awoke, completely aware of his surroundings.
He had always been like this. These days, his body didn't
respond quickly, but his mind was awake. Getting up took
quite a little effort accompanied by grunts and groans, so it
wasn't something to start doing without understanding the
consequences. Instead, he just lay there letting his mind
run free. It had been a week since the Lord told him he
wouldn't die until his mission was fulfilled. Each day he felt
a little less of that initial excitement. Living life seemed to
take a toll on his enthusiasm. Now he had to remind
himself it was real.

"Lord God, I am your servant. Use me for your glory. May
I be open to all you have for me today." He quoted several
psalms as he put his mind and energy on the Lord God of
Israel, meditating on the meanings as he went. He wanted
to be sure he was up and ready, so he could be in a
position of prayer when the shofar was blown from the
pinnacle of the Temple, signifying the applying of the

incense on the Altar of Incense in the Temple. He had started the day this way for many years. It was a habit he wasn't willing to stop any time soon. It was the best part of the day that made the rest of the day fall in line.

So, with the customary grunting and groaning, he rolled over and stabilized himself with a hand on the table. He'd had them make a new bed that had feet and a frame for his mat and blanket. He couldn't get up from the floor like he used to, so he made adjustments. Carefully, he found himself actually standing. The last push to stand completely upright took the energy out of him for a second. He took a few deep breaths to help stabilize himself. He braced himself on the table to help him get in position. He drank some water from the pottery cup on the table. That felt great. He closed his eyes and let the water cool him as it went down. Using a small flint stone and a piece of metal, he sparked up a flame on the lamp, lighting the room in a smoky glow.

He removed the sleeping tunic, folding it neatly, setting it on his mat. He washed as best as he could with the bowl and pitcher, using the towel he had made in his shop. Everything made of fabric in his house had been made either by him or someone in the shop. He pulled out a fresh tunic from the cabinet next to the table. He felt the softness of the cloth, appreciating the workmanship and stitching. He unfolded his fresh tunic, slipping into it with a few groans. His joints didn't cooperate with him as much as he wanted. He smoothed out the tunic to fit right and then wrapped his sash around him.

After completing his morning routine, he stepped out into the courtyard carrying his prayer cloth. He walked to the window that looked out toward the Temple. He waited with anticipation for the call to worship. As the sun lit the horizon, the shofar was sounded with a clear blast resounding through the city as a clarion call to meet with your God. What a blessed way to start the day!

Putting the cloth over his head, he started the usual prayers. He had done this so regularly for so long it fairly spilled out of him. His thoughts, however, were a little distracted. "Will it be today, Lord God? Is this the blessed day?" It was never far from his mind or heart. It was a cry from deep within him. There was no answer. Every day had seen a little diminishing of the fervor he had felt that first day. Normal life had a way of doing that to a person. The anticipation of something wonderful to come wasn't able to maintain itself in the light of normalcy. Doubts crept in ever so slightly, making it easy to slip into complacency. But when that happened, there was something deep within him that argued for the fulfillment of his existence. God was going to work again in Israel. He was to be a part of it, if only he could stay the course with patience. Didn't his many years teach him patience? Yes, but this was different.

He sighed deeply as he stirred himself out of his reverie. He had been catching himself getting lost in thought more often. He had no idea how long he had been quietly standing there. There was noise behind him, causing him to start slightly. He turned to find Elihu standing there with his prayer cloth over his head, imitating his Grandfather with sincerity, his eyes closed, reciting prayers Shimon had taught him. Behind Elihu, Baruch stood in the shadows. He had been praying, watching with pride as his son took his place in the way of prayer. As Shimon saw him, he caught the eye of Baruch. They looked at each other with true affection and pride. This was a very holy moment for them all.

The day started as usual with Susannah putting out fruit and bread. They started their morning meal with a quick blessing, the children greedily grabbing for the raisin cakes their mother was famous for making. Their normal day had started. The shop was waiting for them to get to work. Many things were needed to get done and the day wouldn't wait for anyone. Shimon was pleased to watch them, interacting a little here and there. Elihu rattled on about some adventure he and Micah were planning later in the day. He and his brothers were to report to the synagogue for schooling in an hour. Elihu was the youngest, with Shimei being four years older and Uriah only two years older. Uncle Chaim popped in for a raisin cake or two; then most of them went to the shop. Shimon ruffled Elihu's hair as he hugged him, sprinting off for his adventure. That left Susannah and Shimon alone.

"Thank you so much for all you do for this family," he told her as things settled. "You take such good care of everyone."

She looked up rather surprised, knowing this was what was expected of her in life. It felt good to hear it. She realized he meant it.

"Thank you, S'ba." Her heart was touched by this gracious old man. He was such a blessing to her and the family. Then as she looked at him without all the hubbub around, she was able to see him clearly. There was something different about him. He was softer, gentler, more peaceful. "Are you okay?"

"Oh, yes. I'm just thankful for you and this family God has given me."

"It is us who need to be thankful, S'ba. You have led this family in the ways of God for a long time. We are blessed because of you."

His heart swelled with joy. He knew so many families where God was an afterthought, something you did because that is what you've always done. Here, he wanted to make sure they did things for the right reason: because it was right. Why wouldn't people want this blessing? It was the only way to be.

"Are you going to the Temple today?"

"No, I think I will go to the synagogue and look over some scrolls." It seemed to him that he needed to see the prophecies again.

"Do you want to take something to eat?"

"Thank you, but no. I'll be fine." She smiled at him with that big, beautiful smile he had always loved. Then she was busy again, cleaning and getting more things ready for the day.

He stepped out into the courtyard, looking up at the sky. It was going to be another clear, sunny day. He went to his room, picked up his *keffiyeh,* and blew out his lamp. He put on his robe, adjusting his headgear as he slowly moved back to the courtyard, picking up his walking stick in the process. He stopped by the family room to get a long draft of water before he headed out. Another normal day.

There were several synagogues in Jerusalem. It had to be close so a person could go to it without using up the distance for Sabbath travel. Each synagogue had its complete community. This is where normal contact was made in the community with the things of Judaism. Here the Sabbath was celebrated. The scripture was read to the people, each synagogue had its own copy of the scrolls. Every Sabbath there was the readings. The Rabbi was the overseer, with the responsibility to bring all the things of God to each person in his area of ministration. The Elders gathered and discussed everything (not always was it spiritual conversation). Roman occupation and the politics of the day were common themes with opinions spoken vehemently. They were given access to the scrolls to study. The young boys were taught Hebrew, the Law, and the prophets. The synagogue was the center of their busy lives.

Shimon trudged his usual pace from the house. The synagogue was uphill from the house, about a quarter of the way to the Temple. He took his time so he wouldn't be worn out when he got there. His mind was already occupied with which scrolls he wanted to examine. The streets were filled with people hustling to and fro. Jerusalem was busier than usual for this time of year with people coming in for the tax registration that had been imposed on Israel from Rome. People had come back to Jerusalem and the outlying towns making travel more difficult. The shops were fully bustling with business as travelers were coming through needing everything. The extra traffic stirred up the dust. They were used to it when there was a feast day, but the High Holy Days were not coming for a couple of weeks. Jerusalem nearly doubled in population for a month for

Rosh Hashanah, Yom Kippur, and Sukkot. Having this tax registration extended the hubbub by quite a bit.

His steps were slow and deliberate, working his way through the crowd, trying not to get run over or knocked down. It was quite a relief to make it to the entrance of the synagogue. He took a full breath in an attempt to relax as he blessed the mezuzah on the door frame, as he had done so many times before. He opened the door, stepped in, closed the door against the noise and dust, and just stood there collecting himself for a while. It was dark compared to the sunshine outside, taking time for eyes to adjust. It was musty smelling and the burning of the oil lamps tended to sting the eyes a touch. He turned and walked casually toward the back through the small foyer used to accept the people coming in, separating them from the activities inside. Angling to the right, he went through the curtain. He was so familiar with this place he didn't have to think of what he was doing, it was automatic.

He passed into the main meeting room where the boys were gathered for school. Elihu saw him and yelled out, "Hello, S'ba!" at which he was quickly reprimanded. The other boys were in separate groups. Shimei was close to his Bar-mitzvah, soon to be finished with school and apprenticed into the family business. Shimon slyly waved a little hand gesture at Elihu with a small smile and slipped through the door into the back rooms.

There were others already there, along with the Rabbi. The room was large but crowded with tables, chairs, and lampstands. It was arranged for there to be a central area where they could meet to discuss various topics. The tables were set around the walls, giving places to roll out the scrolls. The main clutch of men was in the center, as usual, discussing something with intensity. They all looked his way as he entered, but it barely slowed down their conversation. He nodded respectful acknowledgment to the Rabbi with a smile as he skirted the main body of those in the room. He headed to the cabinets in the back where the scrolls were secured. A tall, skinny young man approached him. His name was Michal, the apprentice of the Rabbi. He was there to serve in any capacity needed as he learned the ways of the Rabbi.

"May I serve you in any way, Elder Shimon?"

"Certainly, Michal. That would be a blessing. I want to see the Scroll of Isaiah, toward the beginning of his writings."

Michal bowed slightly and went straight to the cabinet, opening a couple of doors, he looked quickly at the labels. He found what he was looking for, tenderly lifting it from its place, carrying it to the table. He placed it down gingerly, unwrapping the cords that held it in its sheath. Pulling the scroll from the cloth that held it, he set it in the middle of the table. Taking the sheath, he motioned to Shimon that he had full access with a wave of his hand, bowing and stepping back. Shimon thanked him sincerely, bowing with his hand on his heart.

"What do you think, Shimon?" He looked up to see everyone looking at him.

"Good morning, my friends. I didn't want to disturb you. What do you need?"

"What do you think of this new taxation? What should be done about it?"

"I leave that to you. I am only here to look into the scrolls this morning."

"Don't you think you have a responsibility to the people to voice your concern? How long are we going to wait before someone does something for the freedom of Israel?"

"Which freedom are you referring to? Political freedom or spiritual freedom? You know what I feel. The political wranglings are only a symptom of the spiritual decay of our land."

A man in the back of the group addressed the man who was seemingly the main speaker. "There he goes. I told you it wasn't going to work to get his opinion. He has only one view for the nation. He is waiting for the Messiah."

Shimon was extremely satisfied with that statement. He didn't want to spend the day in debate. He had better things to do.

With that the main speaker threw up his hand in disgust, turning away and back to the group. "You are useless. You will want to talk when they take away our Temple and our place."

"Maybe you will listen when the Messiah comes." He was glad for this little exchange; it would make them leave him alone for his study. The Rabbi just smiled knowingly and listened.

Shimon focused on the scroll in front of him. He read for a while until a passage stood out to him. It seemed to come alive as he heard the words as he read them. "Yet there shall not be gloom for which anguish is to her; as in the former time when He degraded the land of Zebulun, and the land of Naphtali, so afterwards He will glorify the way of the sea, beyond the Jordan, Galilee of the nations. The People who walk in darkness have seen a great light. The ones who dwell in the land of the shadow of death, light has shone on them." His heart skipped a beat as he saw this happening in the Spirit. The hope he felt was palpable. As he continued he could feel the despair that had come on the nation. He read on as if it were being read to him by someone else. "You have not multiplied the nation; You have not increased the joy. They rejoice before You as in the joy of harvest, as men shout when they divide the plunder. For you have broken his burdensome yoke and the staff of his shoulder, the rod of his taskmaster, as in the day of Midian. For every boot of the trampler is with shaking, and a coat rolled in blood shall be burning fuel for the fire." He could see cities with people busily living without seeing what God was doing. He could also see things happening in the spirit realm as if there was a great preparation going on in anticipation of a grand event.

His heart cried out, "What can be done, O Lord? What are you doing?"

The words continued as if they were taking him on a journey, answering so many things that had been boiling inside him for so long. "For a Child is born; to us a Son is given; and the government is on His shoulder; and His name is called Wonderful, Counselor, The Mighty God, The Everlasting Father, The Prince of Peace. There is no end to the increase of His government and of peace on the throne of David, and on His kingdom, to order it, and to sustain it with justice and with righteousness, from now and forever. The zeal of Jehovah of Hosts will do this."

Shimon realized he hadn't been breathing. As the words stopped, he was aware of his surroundings again. He took a deep breath but stood there in awe of what he had just experienced. The whole message burned within him. As he stood there in complete stillness, pondering the depth of what he saw, peace he had no way of describing came over him. Everything here was all ordered by the Father of the Universe. There was a plan. Not just for the future, but one that was already in the works of implementation. He could feel the joy of God's heart as he knew He was doing this right now.

Then he heard the voice. It was the voice he had heard merely a week ago. It was unmistakable. Clear. Concise. Direct. Loving. "Go now to the Temple. Do not delay. I will lead you."

"I need to leave." Michal looked up unexpectedly.

"What do you need?"

"I need to leave right now." Shimon looked over at Michal. There was a look of urgency on his face that surprised Michal. "Will you please put this away?"

"Certainly." Shimon wasn't listening for an answer. He was already moving toward the door. The clutch of men looked up expecting a greeting or some kind of interaction but was disappointed. Shimon was too focused on something to even say goodbye. He picked up his walking stick, passing out of the room into the front assembly room.

He certainly didn't feel tired or slowed down. He was on a mission. He didn't acknowledge the boys in class, which was remarkable to them. He passed through the room and out the front door without as much as a wave.

Hannah had woken up early, which meant very early for her. There was a peace in the air, a familiar peace. She knew the Lord God was touching her heart. She also knew that today was going to be a very special day. She went through her normal morning routine. There was the usual group of people at the Temple in the Women's Court awaiting the lighting of the menorah and the laying on of the incense. It was time to pray, but she knew she had been praying all morning.

Prayer wasn't quoting words learned in a class long ago. Prayer was communicating with God. Some days it was a lot of talking to God; today was a listening day. She wanted to bask in His presence, but she knew she needed to do more. She needed to be an open vessel and pray for the atmosphere to be protected. She blessed the Temple grounds with peace and protection. It was hard waiting patiently for God only knows, but she had to trust that He had a plan.

She went about her normal business. She stayed close to the Women's Court. This was the first day in her memory that she didn't really want to talk to anyone. She was watching, listening, praying, anticipating.

Shimon hardly noticed all the people clogging the street. He moved steadily, methodically, making his way uphill. His legs didn't hurt like they normally did. He was able to make fairly good time considering the crowd. As he approached the Southwest corner of the temple grounds, he noticed the buildings and walls. It was a very imposing edifice, being the central focus of their entire religion. He had been around it all his life, but now it seemed bigger, more important than ever. He slowly took the stairway to the landing and, after resting for a few minutes, turned to use the last stairs up to the common grounds behind the Royal Stoa where the Sanhedrin met. He stepped out onto the commons and headed diagonally toward the main entrance of the Temple itself.

There was a greater beauty to the Temple today as if it had greater meaning than ever before. He saw the actual Temple sticking up higher than the rest of the buildings and walls. The smells were usually overwhelming with the heat and the livestock available. People who had the means were bringing their own animals or birds for sacrifice. If the animal passed inspection, they were allowed to continue to the Men's Court for slaughter. If the animal didn't pass, they had to buy one of the animals kept at the Temple for that purpose. There were pens and cages to house these important daily necessities. To buy them, they had to have Temple Shekels and Drachmas, no foreign currency. There were tables set up here to exchange money and sell qualified animals for sacrifice. This was abhorrent to Shimon as he knew it was mostly to make money for the priests. "All this will be put in order when the Messiah comes," he thought to himself. He skirted the tables and pens, making a course around the Southeast corner of the Temple itself. These places usually offended him, but today was different. He hardly noticed them. He was making as straight a line as possible for the Temple building. He turned the corner, stepped through the short barrier wall, called the *soreg*, and gained access to the stairs on the east entrance to the Temple.

He leaned heavily on his staff as he mastered these great stairs leading into the Outer Court, or the Court of Women. Some gentiles were able to come into this court, mostly to deposit money in the treasury. The massive doors ahead of him didn't intimidate him today. He was called here by the God of this Temple. He walked in as if he had a special invitation. He walked across the Women's Court over to the stairs that led to the Men's Court. The treasury was on the walls on either side of this stairway. Up the stairs and through the archway was where the animals were sacrificed and taken to the Altar. That is where the priests met with the men, bringing their sacrifices, the business end of Judaism.

Shimon stopped there. It felt like he needed to do something right here. His heart was beating wildly as he stood there waiting. He knew he was sweating from the exertion of the walk up here, but the importance of this time far outweighed anything else. He stood there for a while just thinking. Then, slowly, he turned around facing the court, his head lifted high as he watched the crowd. Everything was normal, but nothing was the same. There was an air of expectancy. The Spirit of God filled the air, Shimon sensed the presence of God that had nothing to do with the religious functions around him. This time was special.

Then, at the door of the Court of Women, he saw them. He couldn't figure out why they stood out to him, but it was as if he couldn't take his eyes off them. It was a couple holding a baby wrapped up in a cloth. The man was in his late twenty's or early thirty's, with a muscular build and clothing that suggested they were people from out of town. Their clothing was somewhat wrinkled and needed cleaning. He was intent on protecting his wife as he ushered her forward. She was young and pretty, a little smaller than most, but was strong, carrying the little one close to her chest in arms that didn't waver. She had an air of purpose about her as she confidently strode toward the stairs where Shimon was standing. Her husband had a small cage in his hands that held two turtledoves. It was obvious where they were heading. She had to present this offering for cleansing after giving birth; this would be the seventh day.

Shimon held his gaze on the couple as they approached. The Spirit of God spoke to him once again. "This is He!" Full understanding flooded his mind. He caught his breath. This was the Messiah! The ages were all coming together. All the Law and the Prophets were being fulfilled in front of his eyes. He was finally here! The scripture he had just read exploded in his thoughts. "Unto us a child is born. Unto us a son is given."

"Of course," he thought, "It had to be a baby!" It all made complete sense. This was how it started; this was where it began. His heart was being filled with joy. What a precious package, wrapped in a cloth, being borne into the Temple. The idea of this being the Messiah in the flesh thrilled him greater than he had known anything would. He raised both hands, palms forward, and bowed slightly in front of them. "Please, excuse me."

They both saw him for the first time. He was no longer someone in the crowd to walk around; he was engaging them in conversation. The husband pulled his wife a little closer in a protective gesture. They looked at him, waiting for him to tell them why he had approached them.

Shimon caught the husband's eyes directly and said, "I know who this child is. I have been sent here to speak blessing over Him."

They were both quite surprised, registering a look of shock. Only God knew about this. Well, the shepherds knew. And they had told everyone in Bethlehem. Word could have reached Jerusalem by now. Shimon read the look on their faces, knowing they could use an explanation.

"I was told by God I wouldn't die until I had seen the Lord's Messiah. He directed me here to you today. He is the One, isn't He?"

"Yes." The husband spoke tentatively. How did this man know? Why was he asking? "We have been through much, but the Lord God has led us here. My name is Joseph, recently from Nazareth. This is my wife, Mary. We came to Bethlehem because of the taxation. She gave birth seven days ago. We are here for the sin offering and to have our baby presented to the Lord as the first born. Tomorrow He will be circumcised, it being the eighth day. We didn't think anyone else knew."

"God knew. What will you name Him tomorrow?"

Mary spoke for the first time, her face softening with a look of pleasure at her son. "We were instructed by God to name Him Jesus."

Shimon looked at her closely for the first time. She radiated a tender strength. Her golden eyes looked out from a face with smooth skin lined with brown hair cascading out from under her headscarf. She was so young, her vulnerability masked behind an outward shield of protection for her child. She was growing up, maturing every second. He could sense a spiritual atmosphere around her. She had been touched by the finger of God. Shimon stroked his long white beard as he smiled knowingly. "His name means 'He saves.' How fitting for him."

He bent over, placing his stick on the ground, leaving his hands free. Bowing in reverence to her as he put his hand on his heart, he asked in such a hushed and humble tone, "May I hold him, please?"

Mary glanced furtively at her husband. He nodded pleasantly at her with a small smile. She tenderly unwrapped the baby a little and handed him to this old man she didn't know. She had a peace that was deep. She knew God was behind this encounter. All she could do was submit to it and let it play out.

Shimon received this little bundle into his arms. The baby had small tufts of curly brown hair with dark eyes. He made little gurgling sounds as he tried to focus on this new sight. The culmination of all the ages rested as Shimon cradled him in his left arm. His right hand was laid gently upon the baby's chest. He felt the God of Israel swell up within him. He let the words of his mouth convey the joy of his heart as his spirit exalted in praise. "Bless the Lord God of the Universe, Maker of Heaven and Earth." He felt the fulfillment of his life as he held the Messiah. The future was in his hands. Redemption had come to Israel in the package of a little baby boy.

He spoke with such deep thanks in knowledgeable worship. "Now, Master, You will let Your slave go in peace according to Your Word; because my eyes saw Your salvation, which you prepared before the face of all the peoples; a Light for revelation to the nations, and the Glory of Your people Israel!" He had tears in his eyes and a tremor in his voice as he prophesied over the Lord's Messiah.

Joseph was awestruck. What was it he said over this child? What depth of meaning! Mary could not contain the impact of what was happening to her child and her. She gasped slightly as she quietly cried tears of joy and exaltation. Her smile transformed her face as joy washed over her. Shimon just lifted his face to the sky, beaming at the joy of the moment. He took a breath, bringing his face down to see the couple standing in front of him, finally remembering they were there. With total respect, he gingerly handed the baby back to his mother. As she received him, Shimon looked deeply into her eyes, sensing the depth of the moment for all of them.

"I bless you both with this amazing responsibility and with the wisdom you will need to fulfill it. May God's richest blessings be on you in every way as you live in God's favor, raising this child." Sensing there was more for the mother, turning to Mary, he spoke with unwavering insight. "Behold, this One is set for the fall and rising up of many in Israel, and for a sign spoken against; yea, a sword also will pierce your own soul, so that the thoughts of many hearts may be revealed."

Mary could barely catch her breath. She knew what was spoken to her was from God. This man was used to bring this message to her. She stored it in her heart, knowing she would need to know this as time went along.

The presence of God slowly subsided, leaving them there in a bubble of peace, which was tangible. The crowd of people that milled around inside the Temple grounds had been pushed away leaving this little band completely alone. Shimon slowly stepped aside, bowing as he motioned them to proceed into the Temple. They both smiled at him with gratitude. Joseph gently guided Mary to the base of the stairs where a priest stood, ready to receive sacrifices and do his duty. Shimon knew he had fulfilled everything God had called him to do. All he could do now was watch.

As he took a few breaths to return to normal, he looked over a few feet on the other side of where the couple had stood. Standing there, with a look of incredulity, was Hannah. She had come just in time to witness everything. She had the look of one who had encountered God also. She slowly stepped closer to Shimon. In a voice of awe, she asked, "Is that who I think it is?"

"Yes, it is. That child is the Messiah. We have lived long enough to see the consolation of Israel. He is alive in our time." She turned to watch also, with her mouth hanging open in complete inability to grasp the fullness of what had just happened. There they stood, watching as the priest received the cage of birds, taking them to the altar to complete the cleansing sacrifice. He returned and pronounced her clean. She then handed him the baby. The priest turned to Joseph, who laid his right hand on the head of the child. The priest turned toward the Temple doors, raising up the child, presented him as a firstborn boy to the God of Israel, dedicated to Him alone. The priest spoke the priestly blessing over the couple, releasing them to carry on their lives. He had no idea who he had in his hands; everything was just a normal day in the life of a priest. Duty done, he just waited for another person to come to present their sacrifice.

Joseph and Mary turned and started walking toward the entrance of the courtyard. As they passed, they smiled broadly at Shimon, acknowledging him as he stood there with Hannah. He nodded his head with a huge smile, blessing them as they passed. Soon they were gone, engulfed in the sea of people, out of sight.

How did one process a life-changing event? No, not just life changing, life fulfilling. Possible even life defining. Shimon just stood there. There was a satisfaction stirring deep within his soul. He was afraid to move lest reality break through this dream. But this was real. He had just held the Messiah in his arms.

Everything he had ever read or been taught about the history of Israel marched through his mind, creating a single thread of thought. All of it became a consistent whole, not a bunch of connected events. It was one solitary story that culminated in the coming of the Messiah. And here He was. He'd had a part in it. Called of God for such a time as this. How could he process all this information?

Eventually, he became aware of Hannah. She was standing just in front of him, leaning heavily on her walking stick. She was frailer than ever, but there was a strength in her, a spark of life that glowed from the inside. He could see she was as stunned as he was, trying to grasp the significance of the last few minutes. He towered over her shrunken, bent-over frame, but the connection between them was unmistakable. She finally whispered, "We have just seen the Messiah. It is all happening right now."

"Yes, it is. We have been mightily blessed to be a part of the workings of the Almighty God. This is the start of salvation being brought to His people. We were here to see it. May God be praised in the sanctuary!"

He absent-mindedly stooped to retrieve his stick from the ground. As he stood up straight, he drew an extra deep breath. It was as if the air contained more in it. The colors were brighter, the sounds more crisp than before. He registered how many people there were around them, realizing they were in the middle of the crowd at the Temple. Normal life was teeming all around them, but they knew nothing would be normal again for them. The ages had all converged at this point.

CHAPTER 6
Fulfillment

Baruch was working with intensity at his loom, developing his business beyond what Shimon had shown him. He had expanded it to several looms with all the other equipment needed to make fabric. He was a man of few words, quiet and intense. His mind was always working, scratching away at problems and dreams. He was as tall as his father but thicker. He looked like Shimon in facial features, gait, and mannerisms. He was proud of that. He respected and loved his father deeply. He had been taught all the most important things in life by Shimon as they worked side by side for so long. He had a strong love for the Lord God and read the scrolls when he could. He had listened to the arguments Shimon had made in their discussions with the other men of the community. Baruch's opinion tended to side with Shimon. Together they were a force to be reckoned with.

Baruch had always wanted to marry Susannah. She was the nectar of the pomegranate, the smell after the rain. He would have done anything to get her father to allow her to marry him. It made him staid and stalwart in his actions, never wanting to bring any kind of reproach in her father's eyes. He felt like he was working for Rachael and Leah, there was a goal in mind. Their betrothal was the moment everything in life became solid. He would never take her for granted but worked at making sure she knew his love and appreciation. It was a rare quality in men of that time, but he didn't see himself as conquering her. Instead, he had won her and needed to keep on winning her. She had given him three fine boys. He was greatly blessed. And he knew it.

As his family grew, he spent as much time with the boys as he could. He had an excellent example in parenting and followed closely to Shimon's style. When his mother died in the childbirth of his brother, he could have gotten bitter, but Shimon wouldn't allow it. His father's love for his mother was transferred to the boys. Shimon had included them in the business early so they would have more time together. Joanna was never really their mother, but they had built a good relationship with her. They were greatly grieved at her death.

Shimei was a lot like Baruch, quiet and thoughtful. Uriah was more tender and compassionate. Elihu was a bundle of energy, hard to grasp; his love of life was expressed in every moment of the day. Shimei was getting close to his bar-mitzvah. Soon he would be working at the shop every day, first doing the menial tasks, growing in the business. He was already doing many things, but only as time allowed. His schooling came first. He was learning the scrolls, how to read, how to parse meanings, the everyday life of a Jew. He plugged along, day by day, not complaining, doing his work.

Uriah, on the other hand, was fascinated by other things and was easily distracted. He was more interested in the common things life offered that contained mysteries. Why don't butterflies fly straight like birds? He was concerned with anyone who was hurt. Taking care of people seemed to be more important than what the scrolls had to say. School was more of an uphill battle for Uriah.

Then there was Elihu. He woke up bouncing, ready for another day of adventure. He had a hard time going to bed; there was too much going on. He was constantly on the go. His hair was always in his face, which prompted Baruch to ask his wife, "With him running all the time, why doesn't the wind keep his hair out of his face?"

Along with that, though, came a caring, loving heart. He laughed readily. Elihu asked thousands of questions, not necessarily waiting for an answer. Shimon was his hero. It was impossible for Shimon to keep up with him, but he would try. Elihu brought life to the household.

Baruch had very good business sense. He was good at utilizing people's gifts to get the best possible outcome. He would send Chaim out to buy wool and flax in their seasons. He was the most outgoing of the family. Chaim excelled in dealing with people, getting the best prices and quantities without compromising on quality. Having Chaim as a brother was indeed a blessing. It gave him more time to focus on the orders they had to produce cloth in various weaves.

Since Chaim never knew his mother, Baruch had become very close to him. He relied on Baruch's strength and decision making. He was completely content to do what he was told, instead of having to figure it out. He had married Naomi later than most were getting married. So far she had produced no children. Chaim never thought less of her and treated her like the jewel of his eye. He and Naomi would spend much of their time at the shop or in the house with the rest of the family. He loved to interact with the boys and take them on outings. Sometimes he would take one of them on his business trips. That proved interesting depending on which boy he took.

Baruch had several employees, besides Susannah, Chaim, Naomi, and the boys, that kept things going in the shop. Each had been hand trained to do their jobs. During wool shearing, they would all spend the time gathering the wool, carding it, and spinning it into thread of various thicknesses. The same was true of flax harvesting. Once it was purchased, they would all work tirelessly in soaking it, beating it, twisting it and making it into a workable thread of various degrees of need. They would stockpile spools of the various threads so they could do the weaving the rest of the year. They had deals with the fuller to make their very white fabric. They had resources for dyes of every color. They had the vats to soak and dye thread. Now they were expanding to make the finer quality of linen. It was hard work but it was expected to bring in a good income for all of them.

One of the greatest pleasures Baruch had in front of him was knowing that his son, Shimei, was soon to be brought into the family business as an apprentice. Eventually, all of his sons were to be brought up in this shop. There was a bright future for them all if they would learn it and work diligently. "If only the Romans would keep their hands off my business," he would complain. The taxes were deplorable, the tax collectors even worse.

He had worked with the carpenter just up the street to make a new loom. It was newly finished and Baruch was working it, making sure it was doing all he wanted it to do. It was quite intricate, but it made some very fine cloth. People were coming to him for all kinds of cloth. The rich people in town wanted things made that were usually only imported. Baruch figured he could learn how to make these expensive fabrics, making more money than ever. It was an expensive gamble, but he thought he could make it happen. Today he was concentrating on making it work. He had configured the shop windows to accentuate the breeze, helping make it cooler in the shop. It didn't matter much right now to Baruch since his level of concentration was making him sweat even more.

He had bought many different kinds of cloth from all over. Carefully, he had taken them apart to reverse engineer how to weave them. This new loom was making it possible for him to recreate the fine weaving he had seen. It would take time, but he would make good on his vision eventually. The piece he was making at that moment was some of the best work he had ever done. There was no room for mistakes. This had to be done right. Once learned, however, it would go quicker. This could set up his family for years to come.

Shimon casually walked into the shop. It was all so familiar that he didn't notice much of it. He came over to where the new loom was to see how it was coming. Baruch had talked to him about it, asking questions and looking for wisdom. Shimon was impressed with the workmanship in the construction of the loom, and the beauty of the cloth Baruch was producing. He had never made anything quite like this. His attention moved over to watch Baruch hard at work. He didn't want to interrupt him, so he kept out of visual range. He saw the deftness of the hand moving the shuttle. The coordination of the hands and feet was a pleasure to watch. The entire shop was working in an intricate dance that had been choreographed by Baruch into precision and effectiveness.

Shimon felt the pride rise within him for his son. Yes, he had built the business, but Baruch had taken it to another level. It occurred to him that the family was well taken care of with a future. Baruch and Susannah were working hard to provide all they needed and then some. Chaim and Naomi were happy and fulfilled. The boys had a bright future ahead of them under the tender guidance of their parents. With the coming of the Messiah as a child, he realized he would never see the man He would become. He had played his part, fulfilling what the Lord God had wanted him to do. His life was a beautiful thing to behold.

And it was exhausting. All the emotion he had experienced today was taking its toll. He was starting to feel drained. He turned without speaking to anyone and walked into the house. He sat on the stool by the front door where a basin of water was placed to wash the feet of those who entered. He leaned his walking stick by the front door, taking off his *keffiyeh* and sandals, he proceeded to wash his feet. He saw that Susannah had cleaned up after the midday meal and was working in the shop. The house was empty. Shimon now remembered that he hadn't eaten since breakfast and was quite hungry. There was a bowl of dates and figs on the table with a jug of water. He found a portion of a loaf of bread and sat down to eat.

The food was delicious and perked him up some along with the refreshment of clean water. Taking the bowl of dates and figs, he moved out to his favorite spot in the courtyard. He knew it wouldn't be long before the boys would be out of school for the day, so there wasn't much time for quiet. He reviewed what had happened from the first time the Lord God spoke to him clear up to holding the baby. Astonishing. Nearly unbelievable.

The quiet was nearly shattered as a storm of energy came bursting through the door. Elihu had arrived! "Hey, S'ba! I saw you at the synagogue today! After I do my chores, Micah and I are going to the Fortress grounds to watch the soldiers march. Wanna come?"

"No, I really don't want to do that at all. I have had a big day and I'm tired."

Elihu looked shocked at that. "What did you do that was so big?"

Shimon was at a loss for words. How did you explain to a boy this young the grand news of the Messiah coming today? You made it simple, that's how. "Well, do you remember how we have talked about the coming of the Messiah? Today I got to hold him as a little baby. The Messiah has come."

Elihu looked at him incredulously. "Really? Why a baby? Isn't he supposed to make the Romans go away?"

"Uh, I don't know what he is going to do exactly. All I know is that God told me He was here and I got to go greet Him."

"God told you?"

"Yes, He did. He has talked to me three times now. He told me I was going to see Him about a week ago. He told me today at the synagogue to go to the Temple and He would be there. Then He showed me which one was Him."

Elihu's eyes were wide open as if he were seeing a magic trick. "Wow! That's wonderful! That's why you left so quickly. God told you to go." His view of Shimon was close to hero worship. His own S'ba was talking to God!

"Yes. We are very blessed to be alive today to see this happen. You are going to be able to see the Messiah work in Israel."

"You are too, right?"

Shimon didn't want to answer this one. "I have already seen the Messiah. It will be a long time before He will be able to come into Israel's view. I am satisfied with that. I leave the next time to you."

"When will that be?"

"I don't know, Eli." When they were close Shimon would take off the last syllable of his name, something only he could do. "It's in the hands of the Almighty God." Then in an attempt to divert the conversation, he added with a hint of false pride, "But I do know His name."

"You do? What is it?"

A reverence unexpectedly came over Shimon. "Jesus. He will save Israel."

It felt like a secret between the two buddies. Elihu would treasure this memory for years to come. He stood there wide-eyed, staring into the eyes of his grandfather.

Susannah came through the door looking around. "There you are. You have chores to do, Elihu. Come on, get to them."

Elihu exhibited a dramatic show of disappointment. "Just a little longer..."

"You know the rules. Work first, then play. Go on. Get moving. You need to fill the oil lamps and water jugs in the rooms." She looked at him with an air of authority, her eyes a little open wider than normal and her head tilted down at him at an angle.

"Yes, E'ma. S'ba, can we talk more later?"

"Certainly, Elihu. I look forward to it."

Elihu was off like an arrow out of a bow. Susannah just stood there watching him leave with her fists on her hips.

"Sorry, S'ba. He's been trying to get away with things lately, and I needed to gather my sheep."

"I totally understand. You would probably want to shepherd me, too, huh?" he said with a sly smirk.

She laughed a little. "If I thought I could get away with it." With that, she ducked back into the house still smiling, wiping her hands on her apron.

Shimon was alone in the heat of the afternoon. Many sounds were coming from everywhere, Jerusalem was not a quiet place. Shimon registered none of them. He was alone in his thoughts.

Elihu had come into the courtyard to dip a small pitcher in the large jar of oil, running off to fill the lamps. Susannah had come through gathering things for the evening meal; it would take time to have everything prepared. Uriah had come through with a bucket to empty the chamber pots; the lot had fallen on his turn this week. Shimon sat and watched the normal workings of the family. He treasured this all in his heart. The normalcy of it all blessed him. Soon, it was wrapping up to the end of the day.

The meal was uneventful, filled with chatter and lighthearted banter. Chaim and Naomi had decided to stay, an event that happened a couple of times a week. Baruch told everyone about the victory of the day, producing a very tight weave of flax. Since all of them were involved in the workings of the shop, a little shop talk was inevitable, especially the victories. Susannah was kept busy supplying everything. Naomi helped her; they worked very well together. Shimei said little, Uriah got excited about seeing a new herd of horses led through the streets on the way to the Fortress Antonia, and Elihu jabbered about a slew of unrelated topics. Shimon watched and listened. He waited until close to the end of the meal to start speaking. It started simply enough, but soon had a feel of importance that made the atmosphere turn serious.

"Maybe you have noticed that I have been distracted for a while. I didn't know how to tell you what was happening with me. I didn't know what was going to happen, so I kept it to myself. But now I feel I need to tell you what happened. There is a change coming to Israel that isn't political or social. I have seen the Messiah."

He told them what had happened in fair detail. It was difficult because of the times when he couldn't contain the emotion of it all. He cried softly through the whole tale, the look of ecstasy in his eyes as he saw something far off in another world. At points, it was overwhelming to him, and silence ensued for a short period. Elihu was reclining next to him. Periodically Shimon would put his hand on his shoulder, inadvertently squeezing it or rubbing it. The only thing he left out was the child's name. For some unknown reason, he felt it was only for Elihu to know.

Baruch laid there stunned. The importance was not lost on him. After all he and Shimon had been through debating the points of scripture, it now all made sense. And to have this happening in his family made it weightier. Could this really be happening, right now, in Israel, in his family? He and his sons would be here to witness the coming of the Messiah. The time was now. How did you begin to understand that? There was nothing to say.

Chaim was taken for a loss. He hadn't been as involved as Baruch, but he wasn't ignorant. Naomi would look at him every so often, but he had no answers for her. They seemed to be there with nothing to offer.

Susannah just stared at Shimon. What an honor for him, but it was also a great honor for the rest of them. She felt so deeply blessed to be part of God moving in Israel and through her family!

The boys knew this was important and very serious. They made no sound at all. Their eyes were shooting furtive glances at every face they could without getting any response from anyone. Shimei and Uriah had no idea what was going on or what to do about it. Elihu, however, knew. His pride for his grandfather was nearly palpable. He could sit under the shadow of Shimon forever. He didn't seem to have a problem with God choosing their family. He wanted to be a part of it all and be involved in any way he could. He wanted in on it all.

When Shimon had finished, they all just lay there silent. Shimon was immediately lost in thought. Finally, he took a deep breath and looked around the room. "Well, what do you think?" No one dared answer for fear of breaking the deepness of the spiritual moment. Then the adults all slowly looked over at Baruch. He was the next in line to be the head of the family. No one else had much to say.

"What does that mean for us now?" He needed direction.

"The only thing we can do now is to wait." Shimon knew that wasn't the answer anyone wanted. It was, however, the only answer to be given. There was nothing else they could do. God had to do more, and they didn't know what it was that was going to happen. They had to trust God. "He will be shown in time. All we can do is keep our hearts pure before God and be ready."

Shimon pulled Elihu close as tears rolled down his cheeks. "We are of all people most blessed. God has given me a blessed family. You are all so precious to me. Thank you for listening to the wanderings of an old man." With that and another squeeze around Elihu, he continued, "Now it is time for us all to go to bed." That brought them all back into the moment. Slowly they started moving.

Elihu turned around and threw his arms around Shimon. "Thank you, S'ba. I love you."

Fighting back deep emotion, with another squeeze and a pat on the back, he said, "I love you, too. Go on now, get ready for bed."

Susannah started corralling the boys, getting them moving. Naomi started clearing the table. The three men just lay there for a while, each not knowing how to respond to the evening. Finally, Baruch stood up, walking around the end of the table to help Shimon get up. It was slow with several groans to accentuate the process. Chaim moved around slowly to join them. Baruch hugged Shimon long and hard as they both felt the gravity and holiness of the moment. God was in this place. Shimon reached out and drew Chaim in, the three of them lost in a powerful, intimate embrace. When it finally subsided, Shimon put a hand on the sides of both of their faces. "I am highly blessed to have such wonderful sons. I bless you with wisdom and strength, knowing how to take this family deeper into the things of God. May you both walk closely with Him. May your eyes behold the Messiah when He shows Himself." Baruch had his hand on Shimon's shoulder, Chaim held Shimon's hand tight to his face. They were all crying with the depth of feeling in the room.

After a long silent pause, Shimon said, "I am completely spent. I need to go to bed. Good night to you both."

"Good night, S'ba. May you sleep well and be rested for the day." They both gave their blessings and Shimon headed off to the courtyard.

He paused momentarily to thank Susannah and Naomi for the meal and their service. "Thank you for being such a blessing to your husbands and me. You are highly valued."

"Be blessed, S'ba. Rest well." Everyone was out of words to speak. Susannah touched his upper arm tenderly. She had such deep respect for this man. "We will see you in the morning." He walked out to the courtyard; she passed him as she headed to check on the boys.

Shimon made it to his room, entered and lit the lamp before he closed the door. Removing his tunic, he washed up some before putting on his sleep garb. He blew out the lamp and laid down, pulling up the thin blanket over him. Every fiber of his being was tired.

"Lord God." He started praying in a different way tonight. It wasn't the usual prayers for everyone. This was a normal conversation. "Thank you for all you did for us today." Calming his thoughts was difficult. He fell into a deep sleep state while he was still talking to God.

The Weaving of Threads

CHAPTER 7
What Shimon Learns

Shimon woke up suddenly. Not like being frightened awake, but suddenly knowing he wasn't asleep. He was instantly aware, with a clarity of mind he had never known before. His eyes were open and seeing, but it wasn't his room. It wasn't even a room. It wasn't outside; it wasn't inside. It wasn't hot anymore; but it wasn't cold, either. He had no idea where he was, but he wasn't afraid. He was looking at the sky, he thought, but it didn't look like any sky he had ever seen. He sat up noticing he had been laying on some form of platform. He swung his feet over the side and realized there wasn't any pain. He felt great!

Then he noticed what he was wearing. It was white! Very white. He felt the cloth. It was unlike anything he had ever felt in cloth before. That confounded him. He knew cloth; this wasn't normal to anything.

That wasn't anything like the shock of seeing his hands. They were no longer old, knobby, or spotted. He felt his right hand with his left, just to make sure it was his. He looked down at his feet. He raised his feet straight out in front of him to display them for examination. They were beautiful. And his knees didn't hurt to raise them like that. What was going on?

In the corner of his awareness, he realized he wasn't alone. He looked up quickly without any sense of danger or fear and saw a man sitting to his left about ten feet away. He was a young man, but to Shimon, practically everyone was a young man. He was dressed in white also, a mid-calf length robe with a unique collar, held together with a belt. He had one foot on the floor and the other up on the platform. His arms were crossed casually. He was about thirty-five or forty, it was hard to tell, with short, curly brown hair and a short full beard. His appearance was enhanced by a full, soothing, welcoming smile.

"Greetings! Welcome. You will have many questions, but first, relax and enjoy."

Shimon liked him immediately. His voice was warm and congenial. "Who are you? Where am I?"

"See. I told you you would have a lot of questions," he said with a slight chuckle. "I am Malachi. I will help you understand and adjust to what is going on. As far as where you are, that is a little harder to understand." He stood and walked over in front of Shimon to look him straight in the face. Shimon could see his clear eyes and knew the truth behind them. "This is Sheol. This is the paradise side of the housing of the dead. You died, and because of your faith in the salvation of the Lord God Almighty and His coming Messiah, you are here. Sometimes this place is called Abraham's Bosom. You will grow in understanding as we go along. Right now, you are limited to what you will see by how much you think like you used to. As your revelation grows, so will your ability to see and understand. What was the last thing you remember?"

"I went to bed, to sleep in my room. I live in Jerusalem with my family."

Malachi nodded knowingly. "Fall asleep in one place, wake up in another. Happens all the time around here."

Shimon was dazzled by it all, but he quickly noticed no fear or condemnation was coming from Malachi. Only truth; tender, nonthreatening truth. Shimon knew his new friend could be trusted.

Malachi put a hand on Shimon's left shoulder, pulling him slightly. "Come, there is much you will want to see." Shimon put his bare feet on the ground, it wasn't dirt. It wasn't wood, grass, metal, or cloth, but it was solid. It felt nice and cool on his feet. The platform He was laying on seemed to vanish like it was never there. He could see no furniture, trees, houses, or anything that was a link to what he knew. He looked up at Malachi, completely puzzled.

"You say I'm dead?"

"Yes. You died in your sleep. That is why you were laying down when you awoke here."

"What about my family?"

"They are fine. They will find your body in a couple of hours. They will grieve for a season, as is common for man. They will miss you, but they know you are in a better place. They know your belief in our God."

They started walking slowly. Shimon had no idea where they were going, but felt completely safe, almost at home here. "The first thing you will need to know is how things work here. Everything is done by faith. Your robe is white, but it isn't cloth." That got Shimon's attention. "You are robed in righteousness. Yes, it is an actual item. Our Father Abraham believed God, and it was counted to him as righteousness. Because of his faith in the God he had covenant with, he was able to trust Him for everything. The just shall live by faith. Because of our faith, looking forward to what the Messiah is coming to do, we are clothed in the same righteousness as Abraham. That is one of the reasons it is called Abraham's Bosom."

Shimon was trying to take it all in. Then he noticed Malachi's robe was different than his. His was pure white, he thought Malachi's was also, but now he saw new things. Malachi's had embroidery on it; a blue, intricate pattern with embellishments of red scattered throughout. The embroidery went all around his collar, down the entire front to the bottom, and around the hem. It was also around his cuffs which ended just above his wrists. It had the same blue as the belt, which had a simple, very shiny, gold buckle.

"Your robe is different than mine. Why?"

"When you first saw me, you only saw white, didn't you?

"Yes. How did you know?"

"Your faith is starting to increase. As your faith grows, you will see more things. That is God's grace so the new souls coming in aren't overwhelmed completely. Everything is new to you here, but your mind can only accept as much as your faith allows. Remember, your body is still in your room in Jerusalem. You are not living in a physical place. You are what is known as a departed spirit. Your spirit and soul are no longer attached to the physical realm. Things here operate differently. We no longer have contact with the realm of men. We are in a contained world of our own. We are kept here by the Spirit of God until the time appointed. We await news of the Messiah. Everything points to Him."

"How do you know of Him?"

"Well, we have every prophet and teacher that wrote the Torah, Psalms, and the Prophets here. We know the word of God. We discuss it, quote it, and delve into the depth of meanings. It is a constant source of amazement."

The thought that there were others here just occurred to Shimon. The understanding of who might be here stunned his mind. Thinking that those who wrote the scrolls he so ardently loved were now within his grasp was almost too wonderful for him to comprehend. As his mind started to wrap around that thought, he began to notice they were not alone. He became aware of others milling around.

Slowly, at first, he could see people, just a few, then more. They were all wearing some form of white garment with every different style and design possible. Each was embellished differently. The people were of different ages, but none were old and frail. Some were fairly young, even children. There were men and women, of different cultures and lifestyles, known by what they were wearing. All were quite robust and healthy, and of different heights and builds. What was most remarkable to Shimon was the peace. No one was angry or shouting or trying to make himself understood. There was a group not far off that sang together, their music was so beautiful and satisfying: it was felt as much as it was heard.

Shimon turned to Malachi. Malachi watched him closely with a little smirk on his face. It seemed to be enjoyable to Malachi to see him go through the growth of revelation. "Why do we look like we do? If we don't have bodies, what am I seeing?"

"Each person is a spirit. Our human spirit is beautiful. But it is our soul that makes each one different. How we see ourselves is how we present ourselves to others here. This is kind of how I looked when I was in my body. I have a certain awareness of what I looked like. That transposes into our way of manifesting here. It changes some as we go along. It shows up in how old you think you are, within reason. There are some who are 'old souls.' They have been here a long time. You may talk to Adam if you desire. Noah, Abraham, Moses, David. They are all here. It only depends on your faith in our Creator. Time doesn't mean much here. We have the concept, but not the perception. I really can't tell you how long I've been here, just longer than some and not as long as others. There is no night and day, no seasons."

"There is nothing more precious to the Father than the human spirit. He created us through His Son to have intimate fellowship with Him. Man chose sin, which plunged us all into death. The Father created redemption to bring man back to Him. The Son submitted to become the one who would purchase that redemption. He is the Messiah. He is the One we are waiting for to fulfill all the prophecies."

Shimon felt like he would burst with joy at the discussion of the Messiah. He had been studying the scrolls for so long, seeing the Messiah just about everywhere he looked. He knew the Messiah was the center of the entire scripture. It was that topic that made him so adamant in his discussions. Very few really believed and would listen to him as he tried to tell others. They were hungry for knowledge about who the Messiah was, when He would come, and what that meant for all of them. Shimon suddenly realized he knew something they didn't. There was importance to what he knew; he needed to bring the news to them all. He knew he didn't know how things worked completely here, yet, but there were priorities. He had become the messenger of God to these souls.

Malachi was telling him about their discussions, how lively they were. Shimon broke into the discussion abruptly. "Malachi! I have news for you! I have met the Messiah!"

"What?" He hadn't just said that, had He? "You have met Him?"

"Yes. He is alive and in Jerusalem. He..." Malachi broke him off right there.

"No. Don't say another word about it. This is something we will all want to hear about. We will have to continue your introduction to Sheol later. Right now, we need to get to the Elders." Malachi's face went from incredulity to passionate joy as he spoke. The weight of the information he had received was dawning on him. The magnitude was nearly overwhelming. Acting almost like a giddy child, Malachi grabbed both of Shimon's hands with a huge smile and light that fairly lit up his eyes. Shimon thought Malachi would start jumping up and down like Elihu had done whenever he got extremely excited, but instead he just quivered.

Still grasping Shimon's left hand with his right, he spun and started pulling Shimon along, leading him somewhere. Everything had become a blur to Shimon. They were moving so quickly, but they weren't running. They were floating at high speed without needing to touch the ground. Shimon couldn't feel any breeze on his face or in his hair. He could look sideways and see so many people sitting, walking, standing, doing no work, not selling anything, not hawking goods. Some noticed them, but others didn't. He was starting to see more about his environment, seeing what seemed to be trees, but not like anything he knew. Grass appeared to be on the ground now, but not any grass he had ever known. Even at that, he knew his feet weren't touching it; he was sailing above it by about a foot or so. He knew Malachi was holding his hand, but he wasn't feeling the pressure of being pulled along. He could feel the contact, though he didn't feel tugging or strain. He felt Malachi's excitement, but he was in an atmosphere of peace. It was all so strange and new to him. What was interesting to him was that, even though it was all new, he wasn't afraid. He didn't understand what was happening. But it wasn't a scary type of not understanding. It was a thrill to be experiencing new things without understanding, knowing he would understand it eventually. He was very excited to learn how to experience all of it. He almost felt a little drunk with all of it; he even let a little giggle escape.

He sensed they were slowing down. They were approaching their destination. Looking forward, he saw a group of men; some were sitting on what appeared to be stones, some were standing. It was a small grove of trees in a meadow. This meeting wasn't formal, but it wasn't insignificant. The men were intently discussing something. A couple of them saw Malachi approaching, greeting him with a smile. "Welcome, Malachi. I thought you were on greeting duty."

"I am, Ezra, but I have something extraordinary to share." Ezra wore a short white tunic, tied at the waist with a green silken rope. He had a light green, long sleeved, outer robe that appeared to be alive. He welcomed them both with a hand on Shimon's shoulder. ushering them into the center of the group.

Malachi advanced through the middle until he approached a man seated on a rock at the end of the group. He was a large man with stunning white hair and a long white beard. He had a single long tunic, with no belt or sash, of brilliant white. It had two blue stripes that touched at a point just at his waist and went over the shoulders and down his back to the hem. His eyes sparkled with youth and vigor. His broad smile welcomed them both into their meeting. He stood and offered his hand to Malachi, who released Shimon to grasp the forearm of this man who grabbed Malachi's forearm in a loving grip of greeting. Malachi bowed slightly to this man who exuded dignity and respect.

"Abba Abraham, I am honored to bring to you my friend, Shimon, who has just joined us. He has something remarkable to tell you."

Abraham turned to Shimon, opening his arms wide as he stepped up to give Shimon a strong hug, wrapping him in his arms in a loving embrace. Shimon realized how touching was different here. When a soul touched another soul, there was an exchange of personal intimacy, somehow communicating a depth of emotion allowing both to know the other in a way words could never express. Shimon felt immediate acceptance, warming him to the core. This man was truly glad to meet Shimon, the feelings were obvious.

Abraham let go of the embrace and held Shimon at arm's length, looking him in the eye for a second. Shimon knew there were no secrets here, only openness and honesty. "Welcome, my new friend. May the blessing of our Lord God be open to your understanding. Now, what is this you have to tell us?" Abraham looked at Shimon with a welcoming smile, but his face had an inquisitive shine to it. This was somehow unique. Very few ever had real news.

Shimon's mind was racing. Here he was talking to Abraham in the company of the legends of his childhood and beyond. He had no idea who could possibly be in this gathering. It was a lot to take in over such a short period. He stole a sideways glance toward the only friend he knew. Malachi saw what was happening, understanding Shimon's dilemma. He reached out a hand toward Shimon patting him knowingly on the back. "It's ok. Take a moment and relax. Gather your thoughts; we aren't in any hurry here."

Shimon realized he didn't tell him to take a breath to relax. He suddenly noticed he wasn't breathing at all. This was information he wasn't really prepared to take in. Too much was coming to him too quickly. He wasn't able to process all this at one time. He was simply overwhelmed.

Abraham reached out and took his hands. Shimon turned his face to him to see Abraham staring intently into his eyes. "Peace." It was only one word, but the effect was instantaneous. Shimon felt a calm assurance wash over him like cool water. He looked into the eyes of the Father of Israel as a calmness rested over him flowing throughout his being until it reached his toes. It felt like it was oozing out of his feet, covering the ground between them.

Yes, he could have peace. The anxiety simply wasn't there anymore. It was okay not to know everything, to not understand it all. All he needed to do was answer the question. He wasn't going to be rejected or condemned. Only one thing was important right now. Answer the question.

"I was in Jerusalem when the Lord God spoke to me. He told me I would not die until I had seen the Lord's Messiah. I was directed to the temple, and there I met a couple with a newborn baby boy. The Lord told me this was the Messiah. He had come in the form of a baby to grow up and learn what it meant to be a man. He had come to fulfill the prophecies. Unto us a child is born, unto us a son is given. I held him and spoke over him and to his mother. The Messiah is now on earth among man."

Abraham was staring at Shimon. He had the same look as everyone there, one of incredulity. "The Messiah? Has come? It has started?" Shimon looked around. Every man in the group stared at him. No one said anything.

Malachi touched Abraham's shoulder, beaming out the news. "The Messiah has come! I knew you had to hear it for yourself!" He had the benefit of having a short time to process it before the others. "I told you he had news!"

Abraham looked at Malachi as the idea washed over him. He started smiling, laughing, shouting. Both he and Malachi burst out in laughter, the joy flooding out of them. Abraham looked back at Shimon with his hand on his shoulder and with the other hand grabbing Malachi's arm. Abraham started jumping up and down in little boy glee. By now the entire group understood what had been shared. Happy pandemonium broke out in the group. They were jumping, shouting, praising, and dancing with each other. Shimon had no idea how to respond to all of this. He just stood there grinning from ear to ear, taking it all in. People were coming from all over to thank him and laugh with him, shaking his hand, clapping him on the back.

Many others saw what was happening, joining the group. The news was being shouted from one person to another, spreading like a grass fire in the wind. The atmosphere was electric with joy and celebration. Malachi saw Shimon in all the hubbub, seeing that he didn't truly understand what was happening. He came over to him, taking his attention from all that was happening around him. Malachi was nearly drunk with the joy, not being able to stop laughing completely. With intermittent bursts of laughter still racking his being, he tried to calm himself with giggling instead. It wasn't completely working. Shimon watched him like one who was not quite getting the joke, but was trying to join in anyway. Finally, with what seemed to be an incredible display of restraint, Malachi pulled Shimon away from the crowd, attempting to act normal.

"You don't understand fully, do you?"

"Not really."

"Our entire existence in this place is centered around the coming of the Messiah, and you just brought us news that He has come. There is so much more to happen, but it has begun. We are all feeling the fulfillment of the ages in the simple news you brought. The culmination of literally centuries of people looking forward to today. This is indeed a grand celebration!"

CHAPTER 8
Goodbyes

Early mornings were always a wonderment for Elihu. What would the day bring? What excitement was in store? What adventure awaited? He knew it all had to wait. First, there was prayer with S'ba. He knew better than to interrupt the Old Man's prayers, but knowing he was carrying on the traditions was important to him and his father and his grandfather.

He sprang out of bed and, getting his body functions taken care of, he washed up and dressed quickly. He made sure to be quiet so as not to disturb Shimei and Uriah. He didn't want them to interrupt his mission. He stepped out in the hall working his way down to the courtyard. He knew his S'ba would be there soon. He stood back by the house next to the door to the kitchen, standing quietly in the dark. He heard his father come down to the courtyard. Baruch stepped up to him and put his arm around him. Elihu put his arms around his father's waist and gave a tender squeeze. Baruch knew Elihu was smiling without needing to see him. These early morning times were precious to all of them.

There they stood waiting for their patriarch to come. The shofar was blown from the Temple, but Shimon hadn't shown up. They were both praying and reciting scriptures very quietly, but both were becoming concerned. Shimon didn't miss his early morning prayer time. He was always there.

The horizon was lighter and soon the sun peeked out. "Stay here, son. I will go check on S'ba", Baruch said in a low, quiet voice. He walked over to the door of the room under the stairs. Opening it slowly, he called out quietly, "S'ba? Are you okay?" He moved in and struck the light to illuminate the room. Shimon was lying in bed not moving. Baruch touched him gingerly on the arm. There was no response. "S'ba? S'ba?" As he bent over closely to Shimon's face, he recognized the pallor of one who had died. His emotions were full, but he knew he had to respond correctly for his family. Laying his hand on Shimon's forehead, he spoke with great respect. "Blessings on you, my most beautiful father. Thank you for all you've done for this family. May the Lord God receive you with great joy."

He stood up to full height, looking up at the ceiling, wiping tears from his eyes. With a heavy sigh, he turned and walked out, knowing the responsibility he had for the day. He came out into the courtyard. Elihu stood there with full anticipation. "Is he okay, Abba?"

"He is in the hands of Jehovah God now, my son. He is very happy. Go fetch your mother." Elihu's eyes grew wide as his face grew long. He ran to his father and grabbed him around his waist, burying his face in his father's stomach. He let out a sob as Baruch held the back of his head, rubbing it lightly. "Be at peace, my son. All is well. Now, go. Get your mother."

Elihu stepped back, wiped his eyes with his sleeve, and looked up at Baruch. Baruch smiled at him rubbing both shoulders and smiling to give him confidence. Elihu stared at him for a moment longer, then letting his head drop, he reluctantly turned and went up the stairs toward his parents' room.

Susannah came running with Elihu walking behind her. She ran to Baruch, searching his face for comfort. He let a little smile come as he nodded acknowledgment. He held her close for a minute, just letting her feel his strength. "We need to tell the others. We have to get word to the Rabbi. Get Shimei and Uriah up; there is much to do." She went up to the boys' room, trying to look like she wasn't carrying a heavy load. She was only partially successful. She stopped at their door, wiping her face, attempting to compose herself. She put on a smile and entered.

Baruch watched her for a minute, then lowered his head toward Elihu. Getting down on one knee, he motioned Elihu closer. He put a hand on Elihu's shoulder, looking him directly in the eyes. "We have been blessed to have such a wonderful man in our family. Now it is time to honor him in a different way. Be strong for S'ba, okay?" Elihu nodded, keeping his eyes glued to his father's. "I have a big job for you. Can you do it?" Elihu steeled himself and nodded agreement. "I need you to go get Uncle Chaim. Bring him here as quickly as you can. Okay?"

"Yes, Abba. I will be quick." Baruch smiled at him as encouragement. Elihu took his mission seriously, dashing out of the courtyard and into the street. He ran the whole way.

Everything was different today. Chaim and Naomi came as quickly as they could. Shimei, Uriah, and Elihu all had conversations with Baruch and Susannah. They knew they were to stay out of the way. Shimei also knew this was a part of life that put him in the position of growing up faster. He watched everything closely, trying to remember everything. He would have to be the one to run things if something happened to his parents. He quietly pondered each thing and filed it away in his well-organized mind.

Uriah saw the emotional state of each person. He was heartbroken. He felt the pain of loss greater than the rest. He wanted to comfort his mother, who was obviously shaken, but had too much to do to succumb to the feelings of the moment.

However, it was Elihu who had a problem. He had to be strong and honor his father, mother, and grandfather, but the loss to him was the greatest. He'd had a very close relationship with Shimon. The emptiness was palpable. It was hard for him to wrap his 8-year-old mind around this part of life. Death was so final. He felt like something had been jerked out of his life, leaving a hole. It had the feeling of being robbed, something taken that he didn't have any power over. He watched the activity through eyes that were dull and unknowing. He was numb and didn't know how to respond to anything.

The Rabbi came with a whole entourage of women from the synagogue. There were things that had to be done and done today. None of it could be put off. Baruch had deep discussions with the Rabbi and Chaim. Shimon's wives had both been buried, so family arrangements had already been established. He didn't come from a rich family, but when the master he was apprenticing under died, he took over the business to support the widow. They had children who had died, one in childbirth and one as a young man. When the master died, there wasn't any family for the business to go to or to take care of the widow. Shimon stepped up and took the responsibility to himself. With that came the family tomb. He had buried the master, and later, the widow.

A family tomb was usually a natural cave or a man-made, hand-hewn cave with a specific shelf where the body was placed. When the next person died, the bones of the last person were put in a stone box called an ossuary. Since a person who touched a dead body was unclean for seven days, this was the time you could clean and arrange the tomb. The ossuary was placed in a niche cut in the wall. There were several ossuaries in the tomb already—the old master, his wife, and their two children, a couple of ancestors from before, and Shimon's two wives. Now Baruch would take it on himself to go to the tomb and prepare it for Shimon.

Susannah headed up the women from the synagogue to prepare Shimon's body for burial. His body was cleansed and dressed. One of the employees went out and bought pounds of spices, herbs, and ointments. Baruch and Chaim went to the shop and found a long piece of linen to be used as a shroud. Shimon's body was put in the shroud with all the spices and burial ingredients; then the shroud was folded and tied so it wouldn't fall open. A couple of men from the synagogue got some wooden poles and boards to make a bier to carry the body to the tomb. Nothing was done quickly. However the house was filled with activity.

Elihu stuck close to Shimei and Uriah. They weren't much comfort except they were familiar. They were all quiet and observant, needing someone to come to them and make it all okay. Soon it was midday. Some of the women had come and prepared food. Some ate, some didn't. Baruch and Chaim came from the tomb all dirty and covered with dust. Their wives both greeted them with no words, just coming close to them and offering solace. The men stood tall and silent with sorrow in their eyes. There wasn't much in the way of conversation. They washed up and ate. The boys took the opportunity to go and sit close to their father. Baruch appreciated them being close and knew they had needs only he could fill.

Leaning back on the cushions, he motioned them to come closer. Elihu practically sat on his lap, snuggling into his father's chest. Uriah sat on his left, getting as close as he could, holding his arm in a tight hug. Shimei sat on his right, Baruch putting his arm around him, giving him a reassuring squeeze. They stayed that way for several minutes until the comfort was translated into them. Food was put in front of them even though they didn't seem that hungry right then. "Be strong, boys. We will make it through this day, just like all the others. Life isn't over for us. It is just a new chapter." His voice was quiet and confident. They drew strength from him.

He moved closer to the food, encouraging them to eat something to keep up their strength. He knew food always comforted the boys, making them feel better. After a little while and a little food, Baruch stood up. "There is still much to do. You boys are doing very well. I will try to explain this all to you later." He walked out going toward Shimon's room. He met Susannah on the way. "How are things going?"

"Well. We are just about finished. The Rabbi is back and wants to talk to you." He walked past her, looking for the Rabbi. He was just coming out of Shimon's room.

"Rabbi, you wanted to see me?"

"Yes, Baruch. How are things at the tomb?

"All is prepared and ready." Baruch liked things completed, and he was ready.

"Very good. The body is prepared here. The bier is close. Only Susannah touched the body. You have touched the bones in the tomb. If you place his body on the bier, you will be the only two to be unclean today. The room will need to be cleansed, but that can come tomorrow. Do you wish for there to be mourners today?" There were professional mourners that would come and wail loudly to help the family express their grief. That had always been something that bothered Baruch; it was very tasteless to him.

"No, thank you. We will grieve in our own way. He is to be celebrated."

"That is fine, I just wanted to extend any service for you we had available. We will go to the tomb the seventh hour."

Baruch understood that gave him barely an hour to clean up the boys, himself, and the other family members. "Thank you. We will all be ready."

The Rabbi left, leaving Baruch to head up all the other details. He went back to the family room where Susannah and the boys were. "We have about an hour before the procession starts. Everyone needs to be in their good clothes and washed up. We don't have time to think about anything else. But before we start, come here."

He knelt, extending his arms. The boys all came close with Susannah behind them. Chaim and Naomi had just entered the room in time to come be a part of this family gathering. Baruch looked into the eyes of each of them thoughtfully before he began. "I know today has been tough on all of us. We will miss S'ba very much and it is difficult to let him go. In your hearts you must all send him away to be with our Lord God. He will take good care of him. We are blessed to be together. Let's honor S'ba with our actions and thoughts today." With that, he pulled each boy close to him in a loving embrace. Chaim and Naomi moved in, putting their arms around everyone they could, especially Susannah. She was showing resolve, but the underlying loss was evident to those who would see. After a few minutes, Baruch stood, effectively dismissing the group to go do what they needed to do, everyone going in their own path.

Everyone had gathered in front of the house for the funeral procession. The bier had been taken into Shimon's room. Baruch asked Chaim for help with the body since the spices added to the weight by many pounds. They lifted the body and placed it gingerly onto the bier, adjusting it so it lay flat and the weight was evenly distributed. Baruch stopped for a minute, placing his hand on the forehead of his father. He whispered words of an intimate nature from the depth of his soul over his father. Standing back, he allowed the men to come and lift Shimon for his final journey.

As they moved through the house, they were the only noise. Everyone waited outside for them in complete silence. They stepped out into the street. All the people bowed their heads, some wept. There was quite a crowd gathered. Shimon was loved by many people and they turned out to honor him. There were several priests from the temple there; they knew him all too well. The priests headed up the procession with the Rabbi following directly behind them. Then came the bier carrying the shroud of Shimon the weaver.

Baruch and Susannah followed immediately after the bier, with the boys in close tow behind them. Chaim and Naomi were next, followed up by the people. It was quite long for a funeral procession and, as per instructions by

Baruch, there was no loud wailing, only the occasional sobs.

The tomb was just outside the city, it's door open and waiting. As they approached, the priests separated, standing on either side of the door with the Rabbi in the street, directly in front of the tomb. As the bier approached, the men set it down on the street with the head pointing toward the tomb. Baruch and Chaim came up, lifted the body, taking it in the tomb and laying it on the shelf prepared for it. They walked solemnly out to the street and turned around facing the tomb. The people had worked their way around the tomb, filling the area. Baruch raised his voice as he did his eyes. "Father God of Israel, El Shaddai. We release our father, Shimon, into your hands. May he be granted peace in your presence!" There was a strong, but low spoken agreement from the entire crowd.

The Rabbi stepped forward. "Lord God, Maker of Heaven and Earth, King of the Universe. From dust we were taken, and to dust we return. Blessed be the name of the Lord!" As those words were spoken, Baruch and Chaim stepped up to close the door of the tomb, sealing it with the latch.

The crowd dispersed slowly. Baruch and Chaim stayed in front of the tomb with their hands clasped in front of them, their heads bowed. The family stayed, collecting around them until all that was left were them and the Rabbi. They had no idea they weren't alone.

The tombs were well inhabited by the spirits of the dead. Death was a familiar feel to them. Many were there connected to their family heritage, crying out their family name to try to establish their importance again. That was their focus in life; now it was their focus in death.

A tomb not very far from Shimon's was very elaborate. A rich man was buried there. There were many spirits floating around, but one, in particular, was at this tomb. Lachish looked at his tomb in intense despair. His funeral had been extravagant in scope and fanfare. There were many mourners and an ornate bier. Much was said over his body, much money was laid out to ensure that it was. His body inside had rotted away into bones; the fancy clothing almost completely gone. No one of his family had died to make them put those bones in an ossuary. His legacy had completely died with him. There was nothing remaining, just dust. All he had to show for it was his misery. He wanted wine. He couldn't get any. He wanted food. It wasn't for him to be satisfied with. All of his lust was still burning, without any recourse to being satisfied.

He had started out extremely obese, but that was only in body. Soon his soul reflected the hunger and emptiness of his new reality. He was skinny, withdrawn, emaciated. He was still naked and covered with slime and dirt. All that was left of his soul was defilement. He saw a procession coming out of the city. Who had died? Was there another soul in torment in this realm?

He meandered over to watch, something here drew him. As the men came out of the tomb, one of them called the dead Shimon. The weaver? He was there before the day Lachish had died. Lachish knew nothing held him out, so he went in to look at the body. He couldn't see anything but a shroud, so he went back out. There facing him was a young man. The emotions were real. This family truly loved this man. He had built a legacy that lasted. What he had done remained. It had eternal value. That tormented Lachish more than anything.

He saw the faces of the family. They honored their dead one. Lachish longed for that love knowing he would never receive it. He cried out in torment, scratching at the chest of the man in front of him. "Love me! Love me too!" There was nothing.

There was something coming to Lachish' attention. Something foundational. There was a light emanating faintly from this man, an atmosphere he hadn't come much into contact with before. He was usually in places where he felt familiar, where the base feelings were dirty, unclean.

Standing here, though, he could feel something that made him very uncomfortable. It just didn't feel right to him. He realized there was a goodness here. He didn't feel this very often, what was it? Uprightness. Godliness. It made him sick. He found he didn't like this very much. He really wanted to leave this alone. He liked defilement. This wasn't defiled.

Lachish moved away from this family. This was an atmosphere he wasn't part of nor something he wanted to be part of — this hurt. He wanted to get back to what was familiar.

He sensed the defiled places were calling to him, drawing him back to them. He resigned himself to going back to where he belonged. He despairingly found himself being sucked back to the areas of town where the wine called to him.

Baruch gathered his family. He nodded at the Rabbi. Baruch directed the whole family to follow the Rabbi back to the synagogue. There was a mikvah there, a ritual bathing pool. They were all unclean because of the dead body they had touched and then touched each other. They had to clean themselves, both physically and ceremonially, before the sun went down. They had brought a change of clothing for each of them.

Baruch led the family back with Susannah herding the boys. Chaim and Naomi brought up the rear. The Rabbi opened the door to the synagogue, letting the family go in first. They moved through the main room toward the right. In the back of the room was a door leading to a tiled floor surrounding a tiled pool with steps going down into it. It was as wide as a man's stretched out arms and as long as a tall man's height. The whole pool was about shoulder height with water close to waist deep.

Baruch made sure everyone made it. He left the women outside the room and closed the door. He stripped down to a loincloth, entered the water, and bent at the waist dipping under the water completely. He took his clothes and dipped them in and wrung them out. He directed Shimei first, helping him take off his clothing, then let him duck under the water. He stood back up and Baruch helped him dip his clothes and wring them out. He stepped out as Uriah moved in, his clothes in his hand. He went under and up and submerged his clothing. Elihu was a little different; he wasn't tall enough to touch the bottom. Baruch took him under his arms, bringing him out to the middle. Making sure he was ready he lowered him into the water and quickly raised him back up, depositing him on the steps. The ball of his clothes was dunked and retrieved. Chaim was there to receive him and help him up the stairs. Baruch came out right behind him allowing Chaim to enter on his own and complete the ceremonial cleansing. They all finished and got dressed in their clean clothes and left the room. They let the women come in and waited for them as they completed their ritual cleansing. This being accomplished was the last thing they needed to do for this day that Shimon died.

CHAPTER 9
Celebration

The atmosphere wasn't like anything Shimon had ever experienced. His understanding grew with his ability to see what was happening around him. His news seemed to release some kind of holy pandemonium. People all around him were shouting and dancing. The exuberance was nearly intoxicating.

As soon as he thought that, he saw some of the people fly straight up in tight spirals, with their arms stretched out, spinning gleefully. Laughter was heard coming from every direction. He spotted Malachi dancing with a group of other men in a seemingly choreographed circle as each of them spun around and the circle they were in spun. It was a true beauty to behold.

In a sudden spontaneous outburst, many of them broke into singing. There seemed to be no limit to the range of their voices, and the harmonies were intricate and extremely pleasing to hear. Shimon saw that he didn't know how to celebrate like this. He had always had a reserved, conservative nature about him, always acting appropriately. Here, it seemed there was no restraint. He could hardly contain the joy in his chest as he witnessed the high level of praise he was experiencing. He had thought the elders would be more dignified, but that didn't seem to be the case. Father Abraham was beating his chest, then flinging his arms high like he was grabbing things out of his being and throwing them up high above him. His face was pointed up in exaltation trying to express ultimate thanks to the God above.

Shimon was trying to join in, but he was almost too busy getting caught up in what everyone else was doing. Then he heard the instruments. He spun around to see all sorts of musical instruments being played with abject precision and intense sophistication, yet with an outward expression of joy from each of the musicians. Singing, instruments, dancing, shouting - all of it blending together in a rousing unity of praise. It all crescendoed into a single tone that vibrated throughout the whole place, as far as the mind could conceive. If he were still in his body, Shimon would have been totally overwhelmed, not able to take it. Here, however, he just watched what was happening, reveling in the moment.

It was impossible to know how long this went on, but eventually, it all subsided into a palpable peace. Everyone was totally still, their souls were in complete submission to their spirits. There was no more ability to express the height of joy they wanted to convey. It just satisfied them that they wanted to. Shimon looked all around him to take in all that was happening. He knew that he too, would be able to do what these people were doing, but that he didn't have the faith or understanding yet to do so. He just felt privileged to see it happen and be a part.

At one point he looked up. There, high above everyone, were beings of incredible light. They were flying high above everyone, looking down smiling. They had the air about them as someone who was tending to their children, looking on, witnessing the joy of what their children did. Shimon wanted to know more about these and who they were.

He looked around him again and people were coming down off their high exuberance with the countenance of peace and knowing. As they encountered each other, they would beam such happiness. They would grasp hands, hug, knowingly nod to each other. Shimon was still lost in the moment of what all had just happened. He suddenly found himself face to face with Malachi. The look Malachi had was next to unbelievable. Such joy emanated from him, seemingly beaming from every pore. His eyes were wide with expression and exuberant delight. It appeared as if he wanted to tell everyone about something, but couldn't find the words.

As he made eye contact with Shimon, something exploded inside him. Shimon felt that wonderful exuberance and exaltation catch fire deep within him. His own soul practically leapt into praise with full gratitude. He had never felt so unified with anyone before. They had achieved a level of fellowship and camaraderie in an instant. There were no barriers between them, only exultation and joy. If he'd had breath, it would have been taken away from him. His ability to communicate this was extremely overwhelmed and unfulfilled.

"How do you express this?" he asked Malachi.

"You don't; you can only try. We have been trying to do that for a very long time without coming any closer to the answer. But this, today, is different. We've never had news like this before. Do you know how long we have waited for this to happen? Adam had been told about how the Messiah would come to deal with our sin. We have waited since then. Each of us has come here and joined in the waiting. Every single soul in Sheol has longed for this time. We don't know everything that is going to happen, but we know it is the culmination of the ages." Malachi stared through the eyes of Shimon like he was seeing him and yet not seeing him at all.

They stood there soaking in their revelry for quite a while. Then it subsided some allowing them to come down from their lofty thoughts and feelings. Even here, that kind of emotional experience couldn't be felt continually.

Shimon slowly became aware of the other people around him. They were mingling with each other, occasionally stopping to smile knowingly at each other. Words were sparingly exchanged as they knew they couldn't communicate what they were feeling. The camaraderie and fellowship were nearly palpable as each felt the connection between them and the equality of position and truth. There were no divisions, none trying to promote themselves over the other, just equal knowing that God had done a mighty work, and they were glad to be part of it somehow. Every now and then another pocket of praise would break out with shouting and soaring. When that happened, the others would turn to them and smile in agreement.

Abraham came up to Shimon as the atmosphere of praise was still continuing in explosions all around them for as far as the eye could see. "How does it feel to be the instigator of all that? Your news is amazing to all of us. Thank you."

"All I did was report the truth of what happened to me. It seems like I can still feel the babe in my hands and the amazing honor to speak over him. I understand this praise, as it was happening in my soul at the time. I thought waiting for him and seeing him after eighty years was fulfilling. You have been waiting for centuries! I don't know how to think about that!"

Abraham laughed. The laughter bubbled out of him like it had been trapped for a long time. "Praise God we don't know time passage here. When you say that it seems like a long time, but time is lost on us here. We just are. But this completion is astonishing. Do you know how long you have been here?"

The idea jolted Shimon. He couldn't answer that. He had no idea how long they had praised. He couldn't tell how long it had been since he first woke up. It could have been days. Weeks! Months! Ten minutes. He had no concept. The look of amazement was all over his face. Abraham started laughing again.

"You are starting to get it. It takes a while to orient yourself to the way things work here. You will figure it out, at least some of it. There are aspects of life here I still don't understand. All I truly know is our Father God loves us." At that sentence, the feeling of exultation started heating up again. They all felt it. Each of them encouraged it. Malachi couldn't hold it in anymore. He launched himself up with his arms held high, shouting praises in a dance spiraling higher. They all were caught up in it again. It didn't matter how long or how many times this happened. They were all blessed.

Eventually, they were dispersed. Shimon had never known such peace or fulfillment. Malachi was chatty. "That was incredible. Just think of what it will be like when there is no sin."

"What are you talking about?"

"Did you enjoy that time of exalting the Lord?" He had a twinkle in his eye like he had a secret he was about to share.

"Absolutely! I have never experienced anything like that."

"There is more. And greater! Why are we here? This isn't the final place for us. This isn't heaven; this is Sheol. The Scriptures tell of another place for the godly. We still have sin here. We haven't had it eradicated yet. Only the Messiah can do that. He hasn't accomplished it all yet. That is one of the reasons we are so excited about his coming. Soon, he will have done all that is necessary, and sin will be taken away. Right now, it is covered, atoned. Then, it will be washed away. Can you imagine what it will be like to be able to honor Him without any sin between us? We have been contemplating that for as long as we have been here. Now we anticipate the end result of what He has promised."

Shimon was dumbfounded.

"I'm sorry, my friend. I forget how new you are. It seems like I have known you forever after having that praise time together," he said with a mischievous chuckle. Shimon could only join him in his mirth. He knew there was so much he had to learn yet. Every second was a vast education.

As they were talking, another person was walking up to them. She looked very familiar to Shimon for some reason, but he couldn't place her. When she spoke, he was shocked by the revelation. "Hello, Shimon. It is so very good to see you."

"Joanna!" He stood staring at her in total unbelief. Malachi was looking back and forth between them. She looked at him with a gentle smile, "I am, or was, Shimon's wife. I saw him when you went past me on the way to talk to Abraham." She turned to Shimon. "Welcome!" She had long brown, wavy hair with a smiling, pleasant demeanor. Her white gown was tied at the waist with a striped sash of several colors; her sleeves were an intricate pattern of different browns. Shimon hadn't recognized her at first because she had never presented herself like this. She had been a woman of grave sincerity. She had married Shimon out of compassion for him and his sons without a wife and mother. It was close to a sense of duty, knowing how it must have been losing Rebekah with everything going on in the country. She'd had a stern countenance before with the concern of life on her. She knew Shimon loved her with all the love he could afford, but she also knew he had always been in love with Rebekah, even throughout their marriage. But here, she had a freedom and beauty she'd had little opportunity to display while alive.

With his mouth still hanging open, she hugged him enthusiastically. Then standing back to arm's length, she helped ease him into conversation. "This isn't what you expected, is it? It is so much more. However, it was your love for God that pushed us to live a godly life with true faith. Your life was the example I followed. Because of you, I am here. I had been lost in living the culture, just doing what I needed to do to get by. You helped me see beyond normal life; that there was more. I have wanted to talk to you ever since I got here. I want to thank you. You mean so much to me."

Her words moved him deeply. He had no idea his actions had meant so much. He had married her mostly for convenience at the beginning because he needed help with the boys. It was a good cultural move at the time, good for her, him and the boys. Now she is telling him it was much more than that. Yes, he had grown to really love her and appreciate all she did. But now he was seeing he could have loved her more. She was nearing forty when they were married. She had been widowed for several years with no children to help her. He was a widower with two boys and a prosperous business. She entered the arena gladly, with many skills already learned and practiced. The busy life had been enough to keep them plugging along. But then the boys grew up.

When the boys became part of the business, they started having lives of their own. Shimon and Joanna were spending more time together without them. They grew closer and closer. Then she got sick. It was harder and harder for her to do what she needed to do. Baruch married Susannah and the households combined. Joanna didn't last long; she had died fairly quickly.

"We mourned your passing. You were a very strong part of the family. I missed you greatly. I buried myself in work and the synagogue and Temple. Seeing you now makes me know you were well taken care of. I am so glad to see you."

"How are the boys?"

"Walking with God, working hard and living godly lives."

She laughed a lilting, musical laugh. "I am so happy to hear that. Coming from you it means a lot."

It occurred to Shimon that Malachi was still standing there. "Excuse me, Malachi."

Malachi nodded knowingly. "This happens all the time here. Reunions with godly loved ones is a major part of what happens here. It is part of the joy making it paradise."

"There are others here that would be very glad to see you, Shimon. With your coming and the news you had, you have become quite a celebrity." She giggled a little with saying that. "May I take him around to some people, Malachi?"

"Certainly. Just be gentle. Remember, he is new here. Much has happened to him very quickly."

With almost school-girl giddiness, she took Shimon's hand in both of hers and started backing away, "Thank you so much, Malachi. We will find you shortly." She kept her eyes on him as they moved off, heading who-knew-where. "I don't know what I would have been like if you hadn't loved me, bringing me closer to the Lord God." Then she asked the question that would be asked of him time and time again. "What was it like to actually hold the Messiah?" Her eyes were fixed on him in anticipation of the answer. Shimon was learning how much this world focused on Him. Their Messiah held all their lives in his hands. This was the greatest thing they could possibly think of.

Taking his time, he started at the beginning and told her the story, leaving nothing out. She was held in rapt attention through the whole thing. When he told of Joseph and Mary melting into the crowd, she finally burst into praise, dancing in a tight and beautiful swirl. Her glee was expressed in the laughter and movement with her face beaming brightly. This praise affected Shimon again clear to his core. He couldn't resist any longer. He also broke into dancing, experiencing the joy that came with the expression. He understood more and more each second.

She came back to him like a giddy little girl. She giggled as she took his hand again and continued on their mission. She was looking around, searching for something. Every now and then she would catch his eye and giggle again. He was delighted that she was experiencing such joy in doing this. She saw what she was looking for and with a little yelp of glee, rushed toward some people standing in a little circle, talking. She turned to him. "I have someone for you to meet." They approached the group and the woman with her back to them turned around and jumped in astonished surprise.

"Shimon! I knew this time would come. I am so glad you are here!" She lunged forward with a hug of elation.

He was overwhelmed again with what was happening around him. What else could possibly be in store for him? "Rebekah! How I have longed to see you. I have missed you so very much!" It was strange to stand there with both of his former wives. They were both so excited to be here together with him.

She was shorter than Joanna, just a tiny thing. She had those eyes that sparkled. How can you have such a huge smile in such a tiny face, he had always wondered. Her very long hair flowed and the tips bounced and swayed with her. Her long white robe seemed to have a train that flipped around her as she moved, the swirls of blue in it made it look like it was continually in motion. "Joanna and I met a while ago, realizing we had so much in common. One of the greatest things we have celebrated was that we had both been married to a godly man who showed us how to live before our Lord God. God put her in your life to raise my children."

"And God put her in your life to give those children life. I had the privilege to know them and see them raise up to be godly men, both of them." Joanna was just as happy as they were to be here all together.

Rebekah reached over and grabbed Joanna's hand, looking at her with such pleasure. "We have shared about our lives, both of us have so enjoyed getting to know each other." Turning back to Shimon, she took his hand in her other hand. "Now that you are here, it seems a bit more complete. Who would have known we would have this reunion with such joy. We are so blessed!"

They stayed there talking about so many things. Memories just flooded in. The two women saw how complementary their lives were. Shimon understood the orchestration of it all in the hand of God himself. To be a part of this made him feel so small, yet overwhelmed with the magnitude. It was too much to comprehend. It made him dizzy.

As they talked, many others came to greet Shimon. People from his life who had gone on before. Each was so thrilled that God had chosen Shimon to greet the Messiah. They were proud to have known him. They knew how he looked for God to work in Israel in a spiritual way, instead of a political or martial way. They saw that Shimon had insight and understanding and they saw the hand of God in him. They were all very pleased to have known him.

One person stepped up that Shimon didn't recognize. "Greetings, good master. I don't know if you remember me or not, but I came to thank you for what you did for me. It was a great kindness and I will never forget it." Shimon searched his face, but couldn't place him.

"I'm sorry, my friend, but who are you?"

"My name is Lazarus. I was a beggar on the streets of Jerusalem. Often you would give me food and clothing. You showed kindness to me when others wouldn't. It was people like you who made my life bearable. Your words at the synagogue and the Temple helped guide me to seek the face of God. When things got very bad, I relied on those words, knowing God is the answer for Israel. Thank you so very much."

Shimon was touched to the very bottom of his being. "I should have done more. What we do on earth has consequences in life and beyond. Why don't we see that until after it is too late?"

"All I know is that you were kind and blessed me. May God richly bless you for what you did for me. I sincerely appreciate it."

The two men stood there for quite a while as they felt the connection between them. This would be a friendship for eternity.

"There are many here you will love to have conversations with, I believe." Lazarus wanted to do something for this man. "Did you know you can talk to the men who wrote the scrolls you studied and loved? I have talked to Moses, David, Jeremiah the prophet. If I am not mistaken, you had a great love for the writings of Isaiah. I can introduce you." Lazarus took it upon himself to take Shimon around and introduce him to these other great men of God. Shimon reminded them that he hadn't been here very long and still didn't know how things worked completely.

Rebekah was first to respond to that. "Don't worry. We will take good care of you as you get oriented to life here. It isn't difficult. You are not alone. Not ever. Not anymore."

As she talked, a sound was coming to him that he didn't recognize. It was filled with joy and laughter, squeals of delight and singing. He turned around trying to find the source of this amazing sound. "What is that I am hearing?"

"Ah," said Joanna knowingly. They exchanged looks with each other as if they had a secret together they were just about to share. "It's the children."

Looking around, his eyes fell on a glowing light that was sparkling and spinning, coming their way. He focused on it in fascination. Then out of the light, he saw children. Many, many children. Running, jumping, flying, playing, they were having a wonderful time. It was hard not to get caught up in their revelry.

"It takes a long time for them to calm down after a praise release." Rebekah laughed with them as she tried to explain. "When children die, our Lord takes care of them. They are here with no more pain, no more hunger, totally taken care of. They remind us of what joy is."

Lazarus turned so he stood next to Shimon watching the children. "These folks are the joy of our hearts. We watch them all the time. Watching them makes our whole lives worthwhile. What an expression of God's love for us."

As the children passed by, it was impossible to ignore them. There were so many! Shimon saw one child shoot straight up for a second and others followed in a loop of chase. While they were up higher, Shimon noticed the beings of light that were up over everything had come down to play with them for a while. One even looked like he was tickling one of the children. That surprised Shimon, who looked at Lazarus for an explanation. "Even our souls feel the sensation of light. It can be played with and used. The light tingles and causes eruptions of joy. It's really fun. Sometimes the children tickle others. They say King David is especially ticklish." Shimon and Lazarus looked at each other and burst out laughing.

"I am really looking forward to learning about this place. While alive, we got so focused on things that weren't very important, it seems. Now that I am dead, I am much more alive in some ways."

Lazarus chuckled at that. "It's so true. Wouldn't it have been nice to know about this joy before we got here? It's in the scrolls, but we weren't looking for it. That is true about many things. God gave us everything we needed. Now, we are able to see it, but not then, for some reason."

"You study the scrolls here? There are no scrolls here, are there?"

"There are scrolls of memory. We see them the same way we see clothing. They are real, but not physical. Have you seen people with musical instruments? Same thing. We are in soul and we manifest soul objects. We remember what they say. The authors themselves are here. They recite them all the time. We talk about them, compare what we heard, discuss things in detail. But even at that, we get too much and have to walk away from the discussions to think about it for a while. We get to meditate freely and bring back thoughts for discussion. Everyone joins in. That is why we know so much about the coming of the Messiah. When you told us all He had come, it was like throwing it all in one pot. It is too much to comprehend. The only outlet is to praise. And we do that."

Shimon just shook his head. "And you say there will be more than this after the Messiah? This is all too wonderful to take in. I am excited to see what God has in store for us if there is more than this."

"There will be more, but you haven't even experienced everything here. God gave us so much that is pleasurable to bring us joy as gifts from His hand. When we were alive, it was the same thing. But instead of focusing on Him and his gifts, taking them the way He wanted us to take them, we abused the gifts and the pleasure they intended to bring. We were dulled in our sensual input and craved more and more. But when taken with thanksgiving, they can yield great benefit. That was God's intent. Here we try to put things back into perspective with what God wanted, to receive the beauty and thank the God who gave it. We even have food."

Shimon snapped around to look at Lazarus. "We have food?"

CHAPTER 10
The Messiah
27 A.D.

He was running as hard as he could. Just wait till the family hears about this! What he had seen was beyond anything he had ever encountered before. He couldn't contain his excitement. He took some of the back streets he knew so well; shortcuts that would get him home quickly. He had been sent to check out rumors about an itinerant teacher reported to heal people! This family had inside information they had been looking for a long time. Could this be the One?

The mid-day crowd was too much to get through quickly. He burst from an alley, almost running over a lady on her way to the market. "Sorry! Please forgive me. Are you ok?" He helped her get stable on her feet with her bags and ran off like an arrow shot from a bow.

Rounding the corner of the shop, he started yelling, "Abba! Abba! Where are you?" He ran through the door, trying to get his eyes adjusted to the dimmer light. From behind the largest loom, a head popped out. "There you are! It's true! All the rumors are true!"

Ezra was a strong, well-built man around twenty years old, handsome with a brown beard and medium-length hair. He was sweating from exertion and slightly out of breath. His face was flush with excitement, his eyes almost as wide as his grin. He was calling for his father who worked at the weaver's shop. It was the family business and his father was one of the head weavers.

Elihu stepped out from behind the loom, receiving the news with open joy. He was shorter than his son and thinner, with shorter curly brown hair and medium-length beard. He exuded energy as one who was continually busy and active, hard to ignore. "Tell me about it! What did you see?"

"I found him coming from the Mount of Olives. There was a good crowd around him already. As I got closer, I heard someone pleading to be healed. It was Manoah, the cripple. He was on his crutch with his twisted leg all bent out of shape hobbling toward him. He heard him first, then saw him trying to get to him. The look of compassion was unmistakable. He reached down and touched his leg, and it started moving! It, it, it," Ezra was searching for words, "untwisted! He was still standing on his other leg when the bad one straightened out! He could move it, bend it, and when he stepped on it, it held his weight! There was no pain. He didn't scream. He just looked at his leg and watched it work like it had never been broken!" Ezra was motioning with his hands trying to recreate the moment visually. The entire shop was now gathered around listening with rapt attention, everyone was held in awe at what was being said.

"Jesus is real, Abba! The Messiah is here! Just like you have been telling us for a long time now."

With his heart practically beating out of his chest, Elihu was having a hard time containing his emotions. The memory of Shimon telling him the Messiah had come as a baby, poured into his mind. He remembered the feeling of being part of the grand scheme of the universe. Now it was much higher. It had taken thirty years, but it's here at last.

"I need to tell S'ba Baruch."

"What's going on? Tell him what?" Shimei was just coming into the shop from the back with an armload of spinning spools. He was older than Elihu and thicker. He was the tallest of the sons of Baruch and had a commanding presence, full of confidence. He grew his beard long and full, with a touch of gray starting to show at the temples and down the sides a little. People always told him he looked like his father and grandfather, with steady eyes, larger nose and upright stature. He was in charge of the business now. The three sons of Baruch were in partnership over the business, but Shimei was the boss, being the eldest son. Seeing all the people who worked there standing around wasn't normal.

"I found the Messiah we had heard about. He has come down from Galilee. I saw him heal Manoah!" Ezra was more than willing to tell it all again.

Shimei looked shocked, like he tried to comprehend the words spoken to him. The knowledge slowly sunk into his understanding. "Really? The stories are real? It is happening now?" He turned to Elihu with incredulity. "Do you know what this means?"

Elihu smiled at him sympathetically. "I think I do. I'm not sure anyone knows it all, but we have been warned to look for these signs. They are here. S'ba needs to hear about it. We need to figure out what we need to do from here. When will Uriah and his boys be back?"

"Not for a couple of weeks, it's hard to say exactly. We should have a family meeting tonight. Elihu, you go talk to S'ba. Isaac!" Shimei called for his son. A man stepped forward, looking a lot like Ezra, but a little older. "Get home and warn your mother. We will need food for everyone. Ezra, do the same with your mother. Get your wives involved!" The rest of the employees were left standing directionless. Shimei looked them over. They also had been hearing about this for a very long time. "Please do what work you can. We will keep you informed of everything we find out. Don't worry; you won't be left behind, we are already behind on work because of Passover week so please do what you can."

Everyone scattered to do what they had been assigned to do. Shimei was a very good and thoughtful leader. He had assigned something to everyone but himself. He put down the spools and stood slowly with his head swimming. Gazing out the door not seeing anything in particular, he contemplated the implications of this news. He had a responsibility for all these people. What does this all mean? What is going to happen in Jerusalem? What if the Romans caught wind of this?

Baruch had moved into Shimon's old quarters with Susannah. He couldn't work anymore, but with the sons doing the business, he didn't need to. His back was curved down from years at the loom and his hands were gnarled and painful from years of working the shuttle, spinning, and weaving. Everyone knew he was the son of Shimon just because of how much he looked like him. Shimon had gotten old, but didn't get bent over or have deformed hands. In his mid seventies, Baruch was old from work and care. It hurt to do just about anything. These days, he enjoyed just sitting with Susannah and watching the family grow.

They were outside sitting in the courtyard when Elihu found them. "Elihu! So good to see you in the middle of the day. What brings you our way away from work?

"Abba, Ema, you know I love coming to talk to you. You are my favorite people!" he said with a wide grin as he pulled a stool close to the bench where they were sitting. "Today, however, I have important things to tell you." The old couple looked at him quizzically. Here was a mystery for the day.

"Ezra just told us that he has seen the Messiah today in Jerusalem." That statement had the expected results as Baruch and Susannah both took a short breath. "He told us what he had seen and heard. Tonight, we want to have a family meeting to hear it all again and discuss what our response should be. Does that sound good to you?"

It took a moment for the news to sink in completely and to acknowledge that a response was needed. "Uh, certainly! Are you sure about this?"

"Wait till you hear what he has seen and experienced. We are pretty sure this is what S'ba Shimon told us about thirty years ago. We have been hearing rumors for a while now. It isn't hard to see when you are looking for it, is it?"

Baruch looked like he had the breath knocked out of him. "What are we going to do?"

"That's why we are having the meeting tonight. We all need to be in on this and come up with a plan. If this is the truth, we are living at the cutting edge of history. The God of Israel is working again on earth. We live in glorious times. I remember S'ba Shimon telling me he had held the baby and God told him who it was. The name is even the same name: Jesus. There is so much to learn. So, we will have the meeting here. Keturah, Jerusha, and Deborah are all getting things ready. They will be here at sunset, kids and all. Ezra, Yitzaq and Dinah, they are all taking part. I thought you should know as soon as possible so you can prepare. We will need guidance and understanding as much as we can get."

Baruch and Susannah were reeling in their minds. Ever since Shimon had told them what the Lord was doing so many years ago, their lives were never the same. They had worked and grown the business and their family with the understanding of the Messiah as the foundation. Now it was time to do something. But what? What didn't they know? What did they know? What did God expect from them? There was an abundance of questions, but not many answers.

"I know this is a lot to take in. We are all pretty shaken. Tonight will be good for all of us. We will meet here just after sundown and eat together. I just wanted you to be prepared as best you could be." With that load of information piled on them, Elihu rose and hugged both of them. "I need to get home and help make arrangements. Keturah will be nearly frantic." With another smile at them, he left them there.

Baruch sat silently, barely breathing. Then, with a full, deep breath, he looked up. "Lord God, guide us, show us, help us. We are totally dependent on you." His hand reached out and grasped Susannah's hand, squeezing it firmly to reassure her. "I need to go to the synagogue and check with the scrolls."

"You already know what the scrolls say, my dear." Susannah smiled in support. She had been his supporter for decades. They were a team, inseparable. She still had that wonderful smile and bright disposition. Her gleaming white hair was a shining beacon telling everyone she had wisdom and experience. She was getting weaker and couldn't do all the work she had always done. The family had relied on her for a very long time, but now it was her turn to rest and watch. She let the younger women take her place and now enjoyed her time with her loving husband. "But you go do what you think you should. I will see what I can do to help Jerusha. This is a good day. God will show you all you need. You are a good man, Baruch. We are blessed to be in this family. Why God chose us to know this, I don't know, but I do know you will do what is right. You always do."

He felt her love and calmness radiate from her. She had always been a rock for the family. How did he get such a gem? "Thank you. I couldn't do anything without you." He stood, having to wait a little while his hips and knees accepted his weight and adjusted to movement. "I will be back as soon as I can." He left her there as he gathered what he needed to make the walk to the synagogue. His head was already brimming with thoughts and scripture. He thought about which scrolls he should examine. He was focused and on a mission. "Here we go," he thought to himself.

The gathering was large, but not unknown. They were a close-knit family and had fellowship fairly often. The atmosphere was different this time though. Even though the children were still laughing and running around, the adults were serious, not in a funeral way, but serious. They greeted each other warmly; food was being brought in, the meal was being set in place. The room was full; the table was there for the adults to recline, the children who were old enough were relegated to eat in the courtyard. Baruch had the position of the head of the table, the place of honor. Susannah was next to him, which was unusual in the culture as the men would sit together and the women would sit separately. This family, however, was an unusual family. They respected the women and even wanted their opinions and ideas. The ladies knew not to abuse the privilege, but had great respect for their men. Most of this was Baruch's idea. When Shimon told him the Messiah was born of a virgin, he knew God didn't discount the female gender. There were still considerations to think about, but their value was certain.

Chaim and his wife, Naomi, were not with them very often. They had tried for several years to have children, but when that didn't happen, they found it difficult to be around all the children and pregnancies in the family. They had decided to move to Joppa, the seaport they used to bring in certain supplies for the business. Chaim was so good at finding the things they needed and procuring them at good prices. He had built up quite a clientele there in the city. The synagogue there was a little challenging to become a part of since he wasn't born there, but after a time of discussing the scripture and having such a deep understanding, he was finally accepted as one of their own. They didn't make it to Jerusalem very often, so they were sadly missed. Baruch knew he would have to send word to Chaim fairly quickly. There was a hole in the family without him and Naomi. Baruch always wanted everyone around and close; it was an impossibility, but that didn't keep him from desiring it.

Shimei was next as the new leader as the eldest son's eldest son. Yitzaq, his eldest, and his wife Dinah had their children there, Phinehas was 5 and Yael was a little over 2. The third was on the way. The other women took care of her and only allowed her to do certain things. Shimei's next child, Esther, was married and they were living south of Bethlehem with their two children. His twins, Rahab and Tirzah, were also married, and both couples and their children were living in Shechem. His youngest, Tamar, was still at home but in negotiations for her hand.

They all knew Uriah and his boys, Tobiah and Josiah, were still out of town buying wool and other items needed for the business, but their wives, Salome and Tabitha, were there to hear the reports for their husbands. Elihu was reclining opposite Baruch. His firstborn, Hephziba, was married and was with child living a small distance out of Jerusalem. Ezra was there next to him all excited with the anticipation of telling his report again. He was betrothed to a wonderful young lady named Ruth, and they were to finalize their marriage in a couple of months. His younger brother, Boaz, was also betrothed, but it had just happened. Elihu had just paid the bride price last week.

Jerusha, Deborah, and Keturah were quite busy, with the help of Salome and Tabitha, with the meal and the children. Soon, they all took their places, Baruch said the blessing over the food and the meal began. It didn't take long before Shimei asked Ezra to recount what he had seen earlier this morning. There was little noise as Ezra began the tale one more time. Even the children could sense this wasn't the time to be messing around.

"I went toward the Jericho road hearing the rumors that there was a teacher named Jesus from Nazareth doing miracles. It wasn't hard to find since there was a fair crowd already. There was the teacher with a couple of his disciples. The Pharisees were also around trying to find something wrong. Manoah the beggar that sits by the gate out there was brought to him. The teacher reached down and touched his leg. No one could explain how it happened but Manoah's leg just untwisted! It was as straight as the other one, and he could put weight on it immediately! He threw down his crutch and started jumping around, laughing and hollering. Everyone was smiling, except the Pharisees, which I thought made it even funnier! He touched a few more people who reported that they were healed, but there was no way to prove it right there. The look on their faces, though, was evidence enough. The joy! The freedom! The whole atmosphere was ripe with joy.

"Anything else a little different happen?" Baruch nearly whispered.

"A man was brought to him who was one of the wine-bibbers that hang around the lower gate. He was that guy that yells at people all the time trying to get money from them. He is mean, and the Roman guards sometimes beat him. As he approached Jesus, his face drained of blood. There was a fear that came over him, and he started to snarl. Jesus told him to be still, and he did! Then Jesus looked him deep in the eyes and with a quiet voice full of authority he commanded the evil spirits to come out of him. The man's legs just gave out and he dropped straight down on the road still looking at Jesus. All the fight just left him. He wasn't mean or vicious or even loud. He just sat there looking at Jesus. Then he started saying things like 'I'm free,' 'They aren't here anymore,' 'The voices are gone.' Jesus just helped him up and told him not to sin any longer. A woman standing nearby burst into deep sobbing. It seems it was her husband and now she has him back."

There was a faint sound from the other side of the table causing everyone to look that way. Baruch was weeping quietly, tears streaming down his face. "Thank you, Lord God. The gift of all the ages has come to us." They knew Baruch was a man with feelings, but this was much deeper than anything they had seen in him before. The emotions seemed to emanate from him affecting each one as it spread through the room. Tears started in several of them. This was a holy moment. There was near silence in the room for quite a space of time, how long no one knew. Eventually, Baruch took a very deep breath allowing himself to calm down a little and wipe his face.

"I went to the synagogue today to look through the scrolls. I have been searching them for years. They are beginning to paint a picture I have never seen before. We have been looking for Messiah Ben-David, the one who will bring Israel out from bondage and rule us from the throne of David into true peace. That is the main idea in discussions among the men. They hate Rome. They want a Messiah to rise up and lead us into freedom politically. I am seeing a different kind of Messiah in the Scripture. It is hard to put together a complete picture, but I don't think that is what the Messiah is coming to do. Isaiah tells of a suffering Messiah. One who is anointed to do many things."

Taking another deep breath, he started looking around the room, gathering his thoughts from abstract to pragmatic. "We need to watch him closely. We have eyes and ears around most of Israel just in our family. We don't have anyone in Galilee, though. If he returns to Galilee, we will need to follow him to keep up on the news." Looking at Shimei, he said, "When is Uriah expected to return?"

"Not for another couple of weeks. He left just after Passover."

"Do you know where he is going?"

"Certainly. We always map out his trip in advance."

Thinking for a while, Baruch was quiet. Everyone was waiting for his counsel. "Let's do this," he said as he raised his head to face the group. "Can you spare some of your help for a time?"

Shimei was starting to get an understanding of the plan before Baruch could state it. "Certainly. Whatever you need."

"Boaz. I need you to go to Joppa. Tell Uncle Chaim what is happening. He may even have heard things since he is at the seaport. Ezra. We need you to keep an eye on Jesus and his dealings. Yitzaq, can you get word to your sisters? Elihu, same with your daughter? Let's get everyone in on this, so we are united." There were full affirmations all around as each one tried to figure out what they needed to do. "Ezra, I don't know how long you will be gone, but we have enough money here to support you out there. Keep us posted. Come and go as you wish. Your upcoming wedding is not forgotten. Tell Ruth everything. After the wedding, perhaps she could go with you." There were knowing smiles and glances all around the room. An unending paid honeymoon was everyone's dream. Ezra tucked his head slightly and just blushed a deep red.

A plan was put in effect that night. Everyone was in on it, and it gelled them into being even closer as a family. Having worked together in the family business had helped them learn submission and authority. They knew how to get things done.

He was not alone. Lachish had been inhabiting several others before now. That was his existence. His drive for the wine had consumed him before he died, but now it drove him without the possibility of satisfaction. The best he could do was to wait for some poor, unsuspecting drunk to pass out. Their protective covering would open enough for him to pop in. Then, when the person would wake up, Lachish would be there. He knew his presence in the man would influence him to search out more wine quickly. The deeper the host's addiction, the easier it was to get them to drink. Hanging out in wine dens was his best bet. The only thing that made that bad was that the person didn't tend to live very long. When they died, the body wasn't any good anymore. He had to go searching again.

Lachish had learned much in the last few years. Visiting his family was tormenting. He didn't want to go there. The world of the living was completely oblivious to the spirits around them. The living had no idea the consequences of their sin. Gluttony also called to him. He found some who had both addictions, but they also had other things. The Romans were good for that. He found he didn't care about the nationality of a person, as long as they ate and drank profusely.

He couldn't get drunk. The wine didn't affect him. The closest he could get was to feel the emotions of the person that was drinking. He couldn't feel the physical sensations. He couldn't taste the wine. He couldn't taste the food. The feeling of a person getting what they wanted to excess was the draw. That gave him a semblance of the former time. It didn't help. He wanted it even more. He was there as the wine flowed into their mouth; he could sense it going down their throat. He tried desperately to remember that feeling.

He also found that he was very seldom the only spirit in someone. There were so many wine addicts who had died so there were so many that when the opening happened, several would jump in. If there were too many, the feeling was muted. If there were too many, Lachish would leave and find another host.

Lachish had been in several people that he hadn't enjoyed being in. Many of the Romans had an addiction to violence or cruelty. Mean, vicious feelings sometimes overwhelmed the wine. Sex was another distraction for him. Those who were sexually addicted didn't get to the wine as quickly. The sex and the activities leading up to it consumed them and made the wine take a second place. The sex addict spirits were focused and over-powering. It was better to have someone who was addicted to the same things he was. Wine first, then food.

Then came the lessons about demons. Departed human spirits were focused on themselves. Demons were something completely different. They were very driven to destruction. They had authority over the person to some degree. They had to be invited in, even though that wasn't hard to deceive the person to do so. There was always a religious bent to them. Departed spirits went for the addiction feelings. The demons were into the person worshipping themselves or the substance. Sometimes the demons would get so into it they would cause the person to do things they wouldn't normally do. Lachish learned quickly not to get in the way of the demons. They were in there inhabiting because of authority of some sort. The departed spirits had no authority. They were there only to feel the addiction and possibly enhance the person to go get it. Many times they would be inhabiting the same person. Sometimes it would help the departed spirit because the person was obsessively driven and therefore, would feel the addiction greater.

The demons were visibly different than the departed spirits. Lachish could see that quickly from the beginning. Living people had a skin of light around them. Departed spirits were people's souls having the visual reference they had built of themselves over the time they were alive. They had a dullness about them that death brings; there was no spark of life in them. Demons, however, looked like humans in the way that they had the form, head, arms, legs, but that is where the similarity stopped. Demons had an atmosphere about them of evil. It was transmitted from them, coming from every part of them. It was like the skin of light the living had except it was a skin of darkness. Their demeanor was always one of destruction, disgust, and fear. They had a deathly pallor, no clothing, and no hair, just a constant sneer of rage and damage. They had ranks of authority among them, which was constant and not fought over. Each one knew his place and function. None of them were ever happy or passive. They had a purpose and they were always about doing it. It was best to just stay out of their way and feed off the scraps of emotion that were left in their wake.

The person Lachish was in right now was a good example. There were several departed spirits, but there were at least three demons. It fluctuated with the circumstances, but there were always at least three demons in here. Their purpose for him was to destroy his life and take down the idea that people in the religious order had something good. The more they damaged him, the more people didn't want anything about God. What made it good for Lachish was that the person wasn't totally violent, but was heavily driven to drink.

Their host had been high up in the temple worship. He had been a priest at one point. Then he had gotten into the wine more and more. Because he was so high up in the temple, the demons were trying to take him down. His family life became worse and worse, even to alienating his children and eventually his wife. He had been kicked out of everything and had become a mean drunk. He needed money to drink, so he had bowed to actually taking money from people, coercing them with threats. Whenever he made people think down on him, the demons would get almost giddy. They were making him odious in the nose of people who believed in God. This kind of activity made people walk away from God. That excited the demons to no end. The good thing for Lachish was that every time he did that, the guilt and self-condemnation would send him to the wineskins.

His host's wife would find him every so often and try to get him to come home and get straightened out. That would send the demons into screaming at her, hissing and snarling at her. The man would feel that and yell at her to leave him alone. She would leave heartbroken, but she never really gave up.

One day she came and found him. She started to tell him there was someone who could help him. She grabbed him and forced him to walk with her, even though he cursed at her and said despicable things. He was just drunk enough not to be able to resist her. They walked until they came to a crowd. It seemed something was happening causing a great stir. Lachish noticed something he had never seen before. The demons had become quiet, even nervous. The closer they got to the crowd, the more the atmosphere changed around him. This was something he had never felt before, either. There was a light touching his darkness.

The crowd had just been clapping and yelling, not nasty, but bright and enthusiastic. There was a man who was jumping around, dancing and laughing, a crutch at his feet. Then he saw him. There was a man standing there with a broad grin on his face exuding joy that was palpable to Lachish. He could feel it, but it didn't feel good to him. It felt foreign. It was good, but it was painful. Lachish couldn't understand what was happening. The demons, however, were actually afraid!

The man with the joy turned to Lachish' host. His gaze seemed to bore right through them all. They were exposed. Light came from the man that shone right through everything. None of the spirits could hide. The host stared at the man. The man spoke clearly with great authority. He didn't yell or even raise his voice, he just spoke. "Spirits! I command you, leave him!"

Lachish found himself pushed by some force out of the host. Now he was behind him with all the other spirits. The demons looked like they were in pain. They suddenly flew away as fast as they could move, completely unconcerned as to where they were going as long as it wasn't right here. The departed spirits were left standing there in complete awe. None of them knew what to do. What they did know is that there was a power at force here greater than anything they had believed possible. They all started moving away from their old host.

The host had collapsed to sitting on the ground with his legs underneath him. There was no strength left in him. Everything that had powered him had been cast out. He sat there completely dumbfounded. The man stepped forward and took his hand. He gave the host strength to stand. He looked at the man with a completely clear mind. The man smiled at him and told him, "Go. You are forgiven. Don't sin like that again. Find your place. You are free."

The ex-host's wife stepped up crying profusely. She wrapped her arms around him, holding him up. Neither of them could take their eyes off the man who had touched them so greatly. "Thank you! Thank you! Thank you! We owe you such a great deal!"

"Worship the Lord God of Israel," was all the man said to them. The wife turned the ex-host helping him navigate down the road.

"Let's go home. It has been a long time." As they passed, there was a man standing there that looked like he was with the man who had touched them. "Who is that?"

The man standing there was tall and confident, full-bearded and obviously a commoner. "That is Jesus. He is a teacher from Nazareth."

The wife was appreciative. "Thank him again for me, please."

"I will."

Lachish heard that without truly understanding all that happened. He stood looking at the scene for a while until the atmosphere was too much to handle. He floated off in the direction of the wine district. His mind was churning with all he saw. He might be dead, but he still had the capacity to think and reason. That was part of his torture.

CHAPTER 11
Shaking Things Up

There were so many people here Shimon knew. There were new people coming in all the time, but it was getting to know the old friends now without any of the old pressures or problems that got interesting. Sometimes someone would come in who was rather famous in the world of the dead.

He spent time with Rebekah and Joanna telling them tales of their family. Getting to see them again was a blessing beyond his mind. If he had thought about it, he would have known they would be here for him.

It wasn't very long, though, after he had arrived, that he walked along greeting people. When through the crowd he saw someone that looked familiar, but he couldn't place her. She was small and emitted joy through every fiber of her being. She had full, flowing hair, an amazing smile, and eyes that twinkled. When she saw Shimon, she let out a shrill of excitement and ran to him, hugging him in a tight embrace. Shimon was rather taken back by it, not recognizing her. He couldn't help but laugh and respond with the joy she was promoting. After a second, she stood off looking at him in anticipation, expecting him to know her or at least guess who she was.

"Who are you?"

She laughed with complete glee, a hint of mischievousness shining out of her eyes. "I knew you wouldn't recognize me! How funny! I'm Hannah! I've known you since you were a little boy. We saw the Messiah together!"

Shimon was stunned. The look of incredulity grabbed his face and seemed to perch there for a while. "Hannah? Look at you! You are so young!"

"I've always been this young in my mind. Old age is a hard thing for those of us perpetually young. Isn't this incredible? What joy!" She jumped up and spun around in ecstasy. Shimon recovered enough to jump in with her. "That was really something our Lord did for us, isn't it?! We got to see the Messiah! Everything we had been waiting for came, and we got to be part of it. We are so blessed!"

"Yes, we are!" was all he could come back with. All the discussions they had while living came to mind. They were close to understanding it, spending their whole lives searching and praying, but now it was coming together for them like never before. "And there is more for us to know and learn. Have you met the elders yet?"

"I've met some. I found my beloved Caleb! We are united once again. I am letting things come to me as the Lord would have them unfold."

"I am sure you will have your time with the elders soon enough. I know you. You won't be able to stay away from the discussions for long." He hugged her again as she was a wonderful gift to him that day. Things were falling into place for something else.

Shimon loved spending time discussing the scrolls with the elders. What knowledge they had! They had been working on the Scriptures, studying them, discussing them, looking deeper until Shimon couldn't handle it out of sheer joy. He would have to leave them for a while just to process the things going through his mind.

Abraham's Bosom was far from boring. There were always things happening. Music sessions with such amazing quality of musicianship to take your breath away, if you had any breath. Dancing times with such wonderful precision would break out spontaneously and pull in a massive crowd. Following the children would take a person all over the place with such fun and play.

It was impossible to tell how large this place was. It seemed just to continue and continue. Once in a while, Shimon would find a boundary limit where he couldn't advance any farther. It didn't bother him or make him want to go outside it. He knew he was here and had no other place to go. Most of the time angels would bring new souls in, every now and then they would just show up and need to be escorted around like he was. There was no fighting, no anger or jealousy, no bitterness or regret. In here, the past was dealt with; it was complete. But in all of that, there was still a sense of something better coming. No one could venture a guess as to what would be better; they just knew there was something better coming. The Psalms had many things to say about that, but it only hinted at things. Such was the mystery of living in Righteous Sheol.

Ezra made his way toward Galilee. He had spent a week getting things in order for this journey he was embarking on. The biggest thing was going to Ruth and explaining what was going on. His family was a very respected family who was strongly involved in the synagogue. Her parents had known Elihu forever, it seemed. They had known Shimon. Ruth's grandfather had been in the synagogue with Shimon and had participated in several of the debates staged back then. Shimon's family was known as a stable, respected family, though they were known to be more conservative in biblical interpretation. They were sticklers for precision and interpretation that showed throughout the scrolls. But that didn't shine a bad light on them. Instead, it made them stand out as those who hold the scriptures in reverence.

Now that Ezra had come along looking for their daughter's hand, they had considered it an honorable match. Both houses were looking forward to the year of betrothal to be over so they could have the wedding feast. Then came Ezra telling them this fantastic tale of Shimon blessing the Messiah as a baby. That wasn't bad enough, but then they thought the Messiah was walking among them. They had their doubts. Who was going to believe miracles were happening, especially coming from such a conservative family who should know better? Then the news happened that took things to a different level.

After the healing that Ezra witnessed, this Jesus had gone the next day to the Temple. He had taken some rope, made a driving whip out of it, and proceeded to overturn tables just outside the Temple where the priests had set up tables to exchange Roman money to Temple shekels because foreign currency was not accepted in the Temple. They also sold sacrificial animals there that were deemed better than the animals that most people brought to the Temple. Everyone knew it wasn't a fair exchange rate, nor were the animals better, but it was a system they couldn't do anything about. The priests were making good money at everyone's expense. But this Jesus from Nazareth came and started overturning the tables and pens, driving the animals away from the Temple. He was yelling at the people working there that they had made the Temple into a den of thieves and it should be revered as a house of prayer. For some reason, no one was able to resist him or arrest him. Instead, everyone working there scattered to the wind. This news was spread everywhere with great verification, and not a little consternation.

Now their betrothed son-in-law wanted to follow after this itinerant rabbi trouble-maker. They didn't know about this. They had real concerns.

Ruth, however, trusted Ezra's explanation. She trusted him more than anything. If he said it happened, it must have happened. She respected his integrity. Now he was leaving to spend time in Galilee. It had to be important. When he explained it to them, he spoke with such passion she loved him even more. She could wait. It would be worth it.

Not knowing where to go exactly, Ezra went to meet with his uncle first and tell him what was going on. Last he had heard, Uriah was in Tiberias. He took the inland route through Sychar of Samaria on the way north. Going was slow since he wasn't in a great rush, just wanted to be consistent in travel. He heard that Jesus had been through Sychar as he stopped there for rest. He heard people talking about the Jew who had come to the city and stirred things by talking to one of their women, a woman of bad reputation. He had told her things he couldn't have known. She told the town, and the town wanted Jesus to stay. He did for a couple of days, talking to them about the Kingdom of God. He had left just two days ago. The town was better for his coming.

Ezra had been told to record things, so this went into the scroll he was writing to send home. Obviously, Jesus didn't care about cultural differences; he cared about people. He spent the night and started off again in the morning.

Traveling by foot wasn't too bad since one of the only good things about having the Romans was they built a road system so they could travel. Travel was pretty straightforward; the cities were connected well. He passed through Nain, skirting Mount Tabor, heading through the hills toward Tiberias, on the Sea of Galilee. It took him three days to make it there.

Coming into town, he asked directions to the inns. There was a specific inn the family had a past relationship with that served them while in town. Finding it wasn't too difficult, but it was getting close to sundown as he found it.

He didn't need to ask for whom he sought, as soon as he got close to the door, he heard his name cried out.

"Ezra! What are you doing here?" It was his cousin, Josiah, who was heading back to the inn from the other direction.

Spinning around with a grin of greeting he was accosted by a young man a little older than him by not enough to count. They were like brothers in look and demeanor. "Josiah! You are looking good. How are things going up here?"

"Great. You know I love traveling, going all sorts of different places. Come. Abba will be thrilled to see you."

Josiah led the way in and through the main eating room to the left and the back. There were rooms separated by doors and sometimes just curtains. The lamps had already been lit, a welcoming glow coming from one of the rooms. Inside there were two other men sitting, looking at parcels on the floor between them. They both looked up simultaneously as Josiah entered with Ezra in his wake. "Look who I found wandering the streets."

The surprise was genuine and complete. Both men jumped up grabbing him and hugging him enthusiastically. The older man asked, "What are you doing here?"

"I am looking for you first. Then I have a mission to do."

"Have you eaten?"

"Not yet. I was hoping you would help me out with that."

Uriah took the reins on the situation. Being the middle brother of the sons of Baruch, he actually made the bridge between them in looks. He was a little shorter than Shemei, but taller than Elihu, with straight hair and lighter color of brown beard. He knew he had to have a fairly full-length beard to look good to his wool suppliers who were country Jews. "There is plenty here. Let's go out and see what the inn has to offer tonight. You will stay with us. Put your stuff in here."

They all headed out to the main room where there was a sideboard with food already placed for the guests who could afford it. They gathered at a table with their food, water, and wine. The banter was light and fun for the beginning. As things calmed down a bit, Ezra got a little more serious. "I'm here on a mission. Something has happened in Jerusalem that has shaken our family. The Messiah has come. Just like S'ba Shimon told about many years ago. We had a family meeting and Baruch sent me up here to tell you and then go find Jesus and report back."

From there he proceeded to tell them what things had transpired. He told of the miracles and the clearing of the Temple. He told what he had heard in Sychar. The report was sobering to all three of them, but Tobiah had a smirk on his face that intrigued Ezra. Ezra gave him a sideways glance every now and then. When he had finished his narration, Ezra faced Tobiah and asked, "What are you thinking?"

Tobiah was very much like his brother and Ezra except darker. His hair and beard were close to black, but his skin was lighter than the others. He was regularly teased about being the "black sheep" of the flock. "We've already heard about your Jesus," he said in mock superiority. "I actually met him!" Then he settled down into the story of it, showing the excitement of it all. "A while ago I was over in Cana talking with our dye supplier over there. His daughter's wedding came at the same time. I was invited to join in. It was quite a celebration that lasted longer than our friend anticipated. They ran out of wine. Jesus was there with a couple disciples. He had the servants fill some water jugs, draw from one and take it to the Father-in-law overseeing the feast. It had turned into the best wine he had ever tasted! It saved the wedding feast, and the father of the Bride was held in honor instead of disgrace. It was amazing."

"We just thought it was a unique thing, hard to verify or duplicate, but now you have confirmed our suspicions," Uriah injected. "I had thought of the Messiah, but was a little afraid to put it down as solid. Now we have more evidence. This is monumental." It was obvious Uriah thought very deeply about all of this.

"Do you know where Jesus is now?" Ezra was thrilled they had news of their own.

"We had heard they didn't want him in Nazareth, so he got a place in Capernaum," Tobiah offered. "He seems to be based out of there. There is quite a lot of talk about him in these northern towns."

"I need to gather information and take it back home. I have been keeping a journal. How long are you to stay up here? When are you going back to Jerusalem?"

Uriah was a little distracted in his thoughts, but the questions brought him back around. "We are just about concluded up here. We should be headed back day after tomorrow. What about you?"

"I will stay with you while you are here. If you will take what I have written so far back to the family for me, I would appreciate it. After you leave, I will head over to Capernaum to see what I can find."

After looking around through Capernaum, Ezra found Jesus's home. There were now a few men who had been called to be disciples. They moved around a lot as Jesus went through synagogues teaching. It didn't take long for people to hear about healings happening through his hands. Ezra talked to many people who had seen things or even experienced them first hand. Crowds were following him around. The Pharisees were also keeping tabs on him. Many had tried to confront him and it turned out badly for them. Sometimes Ezra was able to follow him and see things for himself, but other times he talked to witnesses. Ezra knew he couldn't stay out here forever. He needed to get back home and help with wedding arrangements. He decided to head south after a time talking with people around Capernaum and south.

He caught up with Jesus and his disciples as they were heading into the city of Nain. Many people were around him as they traveled. They were just coming to the gate of the city when their way was blocked by a funeral procession coming out of the city. The family was first with some mourners and the Rabbi. The bier was being born by four men, with the mother of the dead walking beside the head crying bitterly. His body wasn't completely wrapped in the shroud. As are some of the customs in a few of the cities, people were able to see the face of the young man who had died. Jesus stopped and looked up at the procession. His face changed expression; he almost started crying. He stepped out and blocked the path of the men, stopping the procession in its tracks. He looked directly into the face of the mother. "Stop weeping." She looked at him as if he were diseased or something. Jesus had put his hand on the bier, for a few seconds, nothing happened at all as the mother stopped weeping at his command, not so much because he told her to stop, but because his peace comforted her soul deeply. Then Jesus looked at the body and spoke firmly. "Young man, I say to you, arise." There was no sound from anyone in the entire crowd, nothing but complete silence.

Suddenly, with a gasp of air, the young man sat bolt upright, speaking immediately, "It isn't too much of a struggle for my mother. . . ." His voice trailed off as he realized there was a bunch of people staring at him. It took a second for him to grasp where he was and what was happening. He was as surprised as anyone. The men carrying the bier nearly dropped it in fear and surprise. The mother gasped, her hands flying to her mouth, her eyes fully open, staring at her son. She was the first to respond, jumping at him, grabbing him in a full hug, enveloping him completely. He smiled and exclaimed, "Mother! How is this happening?"

The men set the bier down and started helping the mother unwrap him, setting him free. The crowd was stunned, but they started clapping and shouting. Jesus just stood there with a simple smile on his face. The disciples were dumbfounded. Soon the son and the mother were standing together. She couldn't keep her hands off of him, rubbing his face, his hair, his back. She still had tears rolling down her face, but for a totally different reason than just a few minutes before. Then she noticed Jesus.

Everything stood still again as she took a couple of steps, falling at his feet hugging his legs, emphatically saying over and over, "Thank you! Thank you! Thank you!"

Jesus bent over picking her up with a soft smile to her. "Receive your son, good mother. Be blessed."

Ezra was beside himself. He had been less than three strides away from all of this and was shocked into full silence. The funeral procession had been transformed entirely into a celebration that now made its way into the city. One of the procession stood near Ezra so he asked the man, "What was going on here?"

The man just replied, "She is a widow with no one else in her family. Her son had eaten some bad food and took a turn for the worse and died yesterday. We were just putting him in a burial site, putting an end to everything."

Ezra didn't know how he was going to tell this to everyone. The Messiah even had authority over death! He knew he had to get this report back home. "What are the ramifications of this, I wonder," he thought to himself. "How can anyone understand it all?"

Malachi had invited Shimon over to the place where newly arriving souls came in. They were enjoying helping those who were newly dead to understand where they were and what was happening to them. It was quite an honor to bring someone into the place of such great glory and peace.

"Do you remember the day you came in, Shimon?"

"I certainly do. It seems everyone else does, too! I get asked about it all the time."

Malachi chuckled. "It's the smart ones like you that try to understand everything all at once. It doesn't work, but they try. Didn't work for you, did it?"

"No it didn't," Shimon agreed with a snicker. "I still don't understand it. Do you?"

"Heavens, no. The longer I am here the greater my questions."

As they were chatting, Dawrak showed through with a new young man. He was completely disoriented. He was looking around at everything as if it were the first time he was seeing anything. Shimon and Malachi nodded knowingly to each other and approached him gently. "Blessings, Dawrak. Thank you for our new companion. Greetings. My name is Malachi; this is my friend Shimon. We are here to help you. You will have many questions and most of them will be answered in time. What you need to know first is to just relax. Have peace. What do you remember?"

The young man looked confused, but he was respectful and polite. "Greeting, sir. My name is Nahor. I was very sick and in a lot of pain when suddenly I was standing next to this very bright man who brought me here."

"This is Dawrak. He is an angel. His job is to bring the souls of people who have just died here if they are righteous. You obviously are looking forward to the coming Messiah, that is why he brought you here."

Dawrak bowed in reverence, smiled simply, and started backing away while he floated upwards. Turning slowly, he picked up speed and disappeared beyond the barrier.

"He doesn't talk much, but believe me, he has plenty to say." Malachi just watched where Dawrak had gone with his hands on his hips. "I got him talking one day. What he knows is amazing. He has seen so much. But he is positively taciturn most of the time." Turning back to Nahor shaking his head, he then changed the subject and looked at his new young charge. "So take your time. Everything is new and different. You died. This is called Abraham's Bosom or, to some, Paradise. You don't have a body anymore; you are spirit and soul. You will never again be in pain or sorrow." As he talked, they slowly started walking.

Malachi just kept talking softly, letting Nahor ask questions when he needed to. Shimon walked with them, off to the side, being moral support. Obviously, Malachi didn't need any help. Who knew how long he had been doing this. He didn't. Time meant nothing here.

They kept walking along. Nahor's robe was starting to show color. He was only twelve years old when he died. He had a maturity about him learned from needing to grow up too fast, taking responsibility for his family too early. An angel from above them came floating down closer, signaling to Malachi to bring Nahor over to this certain group of people. The angel alighted behind a certain man who turned to hear from him. This is how certain information was distributed from the Lord to the people. The man listened and then deeply reacted to the information. With a look of extreme joy on his face, he spun around and looked at Nahor.

"Welcome," he said brightly but obviously holding himself back. "I know you don't know me, but I am your father."

Nahor stood totally speechless. He had no idea how to respond to that. The man turned to Malachi. "Please, forgive me. My name is Ribai. I died in a storm on the Sea of Galilee. My family lives in Nain. I have just been informed that this is Nahor. My Nahor." Turning back to Nahor, he grabbed both of his hands looking him straight in the face. "I know it must have been hard growing up without a father. I'm sure your mother loved you greatly. But why are you here? I am very glad to see you, but you are so young. I didn't expect you so soon."

Still very shaken, Nahor started telling his Father about how they had been living. "We have had a very small living. We have been cared for by friends. None of the family is around us. I was being groomed to start as an apprentice to the stonemason, since he had no family of his own. Then I ate something that made me sick. I get sicker and sicker. The pain was so strong. And the fever was so bad. I am hoping—"

His sentence was abruptly interrupted. Almost faster than any one of them could register it, Nahor was snatched away. They all heard a voice in the distance saying, "Young man. I tell you, arise." One second he was there with them, the next he had flown up through the barrier and was gone. Every one of them was shocked beyond response. They didn't know what to do. They stood there staring at each other, looking for answers, without having any.

The angel that had come to Ribai, came floating down to the group. They looked up to him with expressions of inquisition. The angel smiled at them. "Peace to you. The Master has called the young man to come back. He was raised from the dead and presented back to his mother. He won't be coming back for a while."

All of them were stunned. This hadn't happened before that any of them had known. Ribai was the first to respond. "That is awesome! He is back to take care of his mother! But I got to meet him anyway! Praise to our God in the Highest!" He began jumping and running and praising, out of control. This was high praise indeed.

Malachi got that look one gets when someone plays a good joke on them and gets them good. He laughed, shaking his head. "That was great. We have evidence of what the Messiah is doing. He is raising the dead! Amazing."

Shimon, however, had a different response. It shook him to the core. "This means someone can be taken from here and put back in life." He didn't know why someone would want that, but now the thought was stuck in his head. He felt highly honored to have been of the few who had witnessed this. But it got him thinking of things he had no idea he could think about.

It was Malachi who brought him back. "I guess we should go tell this to the Elders, don't you think?" He started walking. Shimon fell in step with him. This was a truly remarkable day.

Jerusalem never changed. It looked, smelled, felt, and sounded just as it did before he left. Ezra found a little comfort in that idea. With everything else changing, it was good to know some things were the same. It had been almost six months since he left. His returning was a lot later than he had wanted, but he didn't want to put his whole life on hold. He had been writing Ruth and the family fairly consistently. They had written back, so communication wasn't lacking too badly. But communications wasn't a total relationship. Ezra missed Ruth.

He went first to the shop. He wanted to report in and drop off the scrolls of journals. This new development of raising the dead had not been reported, yet. That should stir things up a little.

The shop was bustling with activity. Looms were clacking, people were moving around, voices were calling out for materials, and the general hubbub of business as things steadily moved on. He walked in and stealthily peeked around the corner displaying his grinning head to the operator. "Hi. Miss me?" Elihu jumped in surprise.

"Ezra! You're back!" Elihu stopped in mid-shuttle, abandoning everything, bounded off his stool, and ran over to his son. Their embrace was tight, strong, and lasting. "We have missed you so much. Have you seen your mother?"

"No. Just got here. I wanted to clean up before I went to see Ruth. Is E'ma here?"

"Yes, she is here somewhere. Keturah! Keturah! Come quickly!" Out of the back rooms, Keturah came wiping her hands on her apron a look of concern on her face. When she saw Ezra, everything changed. She ran to him, holding him tight and kissing his face.

"I am so glad you have come home. How have you been? Have you been eating well? You look thinner." Mothers are mothers everywhere in the world.

"I'm doing very well. I am hungry, though, now that you mention it."

Their excitement got the attention of the entire shop that came grinding to a halt. Nothing was going to get done for a little while. From behind another loom came Shimei smiling a heartfelt greeting. "Good to have you home. I have loved your reports. Uriah told us about some of your things and what had happened to them. When can you tell us what you know?"

"Tonight, please. I want to go see Ruth. I need to see if we are going to get married or not!" Everyone smiled at that.

"Go. Get settled and cleaned up. Let's bring everyone in for dinner tonight." Shimei just put out an order, and everyone understood it. Being mid-afternoon left very little time to get things together, but this family was good at this. People knew their jobs, both in the business and in the family. Everyone scattered to do what they needed to do, except Keturah. She wasn't going to be separated from her son that easily. He needed food!

The evening meal was more crowded than last time since Uriah and his sons were there. This room was filled. The meal went well; everyone had plenty with leftovers. Baruch was in place with anticipation oozing out of him. He was patient, but it wasn't easy. Finally, the preliminaries had been taken care of, it was time to get down to the matters at hand.

"Come, Ezra. Tell us what you know." Ezra moved around to sit on a stool so everyone could see him. His report held everyone's attention. He told of the city of Sychar, the home of Jesus in Capernaum, and the eyewitness accounts he had gathered; so many healings he had heard of and some he had seen. He detailed the teachings he had heard and the sermon that had been given to a huge crowd on the shore of Galilee. Every piece of news he could think of was given to the family, except the last one. He was waiting for the right time. Then as the feeling of awe had risen almost to a peak, he told them about raising the dead son of the widow in Nain. It felt like the atmosphere could be palpably cut with a knife. His narrative had done its job.

Baruch had forgotten how to breathe until a sob burst out from him. There was barely a dry eye in the room. Elihu broke into Psalms of praise, his face covered in tears. Uriah just knelt there with his eyes shut rocking back and forth with his hands held high. This lasted until his emotions subsided.

One person in the room that didn't know what to do was Ruth. Ezra had brought her. She had enjoyed the meal and the fellowship with the family members. She had helped in the kitchen and in serving. It all seemed familiar to her, except her family wasn't this large. When Ezra's report came, she was totally overwhelmed. She watched each of them during the report. Her mind was racing trying to understand what was happening in the room. The only thing she could relate it to was the religious meeting she had been to, but not allowed to participate in. She had been told to be in the background; it was for men only. Ezra had tried to explain to her they believed in God wanting a relationship with both men and women. She didn't understand it back then, she was having a real struggle with it now. She saw how the women were also crying good tears and how the men didn't hold anything back in front of them. She had no idea how to process this information. Her life had just taken a drastic turn, but it seemed to be a good thing.

As the atmosphere calmed down, everyone sat there looking at each other trying to get a handle on all of this. Ezra left his stool and returned to his place at the table having a little wine to rehydrate his throat. Ruth just stared at him. That caught his eye. Looking up at her, he smiled knowingly. That smile supported her in a way she couldn't explain. "This is a man to hang onto. He knows life and will bring it to his family." Her thoughts sealed her love for him.

Baruch brought everyone back to the room by asking, "Well, what do we do now?"

Elihu was the one to bring up what was needed. "We have a wedding to plan, for one. We will be able to get word about Jesus fairly easily now. Everyone is hearing about him and we will be able to follow him here. We don't know what the future holds and for how long. Let's just live and wait. We will be ready for whatever happens."

"If we hear about something we need to examine further, we can send someone." Shimei was following what Elihu said. "Uriah will be going out purchasing materials. That should keep us informed fairly well. He can send word."

The family was in agreement. They knew God had given them this news years ago and that it was a huge gift. They wanted to respond to the gift in the right way. Each of them knew that they had experienced something beyond their ability to understand. Every once in a while, they would glance at each other and smile knowingly.

Righteous Sheol was different, for some reason. Ever since Nahor had been taken back, the discussions were about that and what it might have meant. All they really knew was it showed the Messiah's authority over death. What that meant was beyond any of them.

Shimon and Malachi were having some very interesting discussions. Malachi talked about the difference of being alive and being dead. It was a unique point of view coming from someone who had experienced both. So had Shimon, but he hadn't been around as long as Malachi had.

"Don't you think it was interesting how no one here knew about this 'raising the dead' thing?" Malachi mused. He stared off into the distance, not focusing on anything in particular. "I mean, we have here everyone who God used to write the scripture so far. They were each of them empowered by the Holy Spirit to speak and write. But in here, we aren't hearing from God about anything. But we know we are closer to him than ever."

"It has been interesting to talk to them. Talking to Isaiah is fun. He had the most prophecies about the Messiah. He is the one I read on a regular basis. What is funny is, that he doesn't necessarily know more about it than we do. He got some revelation, but mostly he just wrote it down."

"Funny. You never asked me."

"Asked you what?"

"What revelation I got."

Shimon was now looking at him with a very serious expression. "What do you mean?"

"I wrote the book of Malachi. Haven't you put that together yet?"

Stunned. Shocked. Shimon was just staring at him like he had only just now saw him. "You? You wrote Malachi? Why didn't you tell me that before?"

"You never asked!"

Shimon tilted his head and raised one eyebrow. "Really?"

Right then, just above them, Dawrak brought in a little girl, maybe 8 or 9 years old, but didn't land. Malachi looked up at him just a few feet above them. "Dawrak. What is happening?"

"I am not allowed to release her yet."

That got their attention. They were both totally attentive on him now. The girl was looking around, but still within arm's reach of Dawrak. She was peaceful and quiet. He slowly took her over to a group of women who were not far off. Dawrak landed with the little girl. The women all gathered around her, making her feel welcome and warm. All the women sat down around her, one of them pulling her close and letting her sit on her lap. The girl looked a little bewildered. The woman spoke to her very gently. "It's alright. You are safe."

"Where's my Abba? My E'ma? Where am I?" Her voice was tiny and quiet, she searched the lady's eyes and face for something familiar.

"They are okay. You are okay. You are being kept here for a while. All is well."

"I don't feel bad anymore. Is my sickness gone?"

"Yes, my child. It is all gone. You are in a safe place."

This went on for a while. They talked about all sorts of things. The whole while, Dawrak was right there. Shimon and Malachi watched without speaking a word. Something about this was different. It was a holy moment.

Then a knowing look came over Dawrak, and he smiled. "Oh, not delivery, escort. Be blessed, my friends." With that, he turned and took her up in a blinding display of light and speed. Everyone was taken aback by that.

"What? Again?" Shimon was beside himself.

They heard the voice in the atmosphere again, "Little girl, I say to you. Rise up."

The woman who had been with the little girl was praising and laughing. "That was my great grand-daughter. What a blessing. She is no longer sick."

Shimon and Malachi could do nothing but look at each other.

CHAPTER 12
Life and Death

The wedding was splendid and breathtaking. It was everything Elihu and Keturah had ever wanted for one of their sons. Their eldest child was a girl, and that was great and they highly honored her at her wedding, but to see the family line continue was a blessing and an honor. They made sure everyone knew that.

Ezra and Ruth's engagement was long for normal cultural timings it should have been a year, but with Ezra gone for so long, it was postponed for a while. It didn't really matter. Ruth was more than excited to be married into this family. The night of the meeting when Ezra returned was more than enough to set that in place. She had loved him before, but now it had a depth and purpose with a future she hadn't known was possible.

They had built another room on the back of Elihu's house. When Baruch had taken over as the patriarch of the family, he had taken over the house of Shimon. Shimei lived there with his family, who filled it quite completely. Uriah had built up enough money to buy a place not far away, and his sons both built rooms on it for them and their wives and growing families. Elihu did the same. His place was even closer to the shop and Baruch's house. An older couple who had no children to inherit it sold it to him. They had room to expand, and now Ezra and Ruth were moving in. The prospects of a growing family were exciting to them all. It was wonderful to have a good and godly relationship with your children. Soon they would have Boaz and his wife moving in, too. How blessed they all were.

Since they were all in the business together, it wasn't hard to get a lot of people to come to the wedding feast: there were many, many guests from all over. Baruch and Shimei were the heads of the business during all these years, and Elihu had his own sphere of influence. All of these people wanted to come to bless the family. Add all of Ruth's family, and it was quite an affair.

Ezra was dressed in freshly made garments that were rich and glorious. His whole family and friends made the Groom's processional with trumpets, tambourines, torches and lamps, and dancing. They went from Elihu's house just after sundown and wound down through the streets making all sorts of noise. They made it to Ruth's family home after dark with shouts of "bring out the bride!" and blessings on her family. Ruth came out with her bridal party. She was dressed in a beautiful white linen dress with a head covering that matched. She had a band of flowers and ribbons wrapped around her head holding on the head piece. Her delicate face and beaming smile could just be seen under it all. Her long hair spilled out over her shoulders from around her neck giving a light brown accent in the sea of white. She was a beauty to remember.

They carried Ezra and Ruth on special litters back through the streets to Elihu's house where a huge place was set up to feed all the guests. The rabbi officiated over the making of the covenant vows and the joining of the two families as he placed on her head the string of covenant coins that graced her forehead. She was adorned for the rest of the ceremony. There was much wine and food. It stuck in the back of Ezra's mind how Jesus had turned water into wine to satisfy a wedding such as this. He knew, however, Elihu would make sure there were no shortages.

After all the hoopla was ended, Ezra and Ruth made their way to their rooms in the back amid shouts and blessings. The party continued for a time as the rabbi and Elihu waited knowingly until the token of virginity was passed out through their door. It was proclaimed a valid marriage by them both and another round of shouting and dancing exploded. Then the party was over; the guests could go their way; everything had been satisfied.

That had been three months ago. Life had continued. Ezra and Ruth had emerged as a real married couple and had begun life as real people. But, in the middle of all this, the reports from all over kept coming in. People all over the nation had heard through the family dealings they were interested in what Jesus was doing. When folks heard something, they sent word to Shimei's shop. The stories were getting wild. The scandalous ones about doing things on the Sabbath took everyone by surprise. The raising of disciples had taken a much bigger place with over seventy being counted. Then they heard of most of the new disciples leaving the group angry. They had many discussions in the shop about the goings on, but even though bewildered, they didn't lose hope or faith. They heard from Pharisees on both sides of the controversies. Their own synagogue was divided. Everyone knew where this family stood. Some of the family related by marriage was on the other side. The family of the girl Boaz had become betrothed to had withdrawn and broke off their betrothal. It made the family even more adamant. It amazed Baruch how estranged some people were getting over it. The Sanhedrin, the ruling body over Israel, was mostly against Jesus, but there were those on the council that were secret proponents of him. Most of the priesthood were politically aligned with the Pharisees, making things at the Temple a little tricky. Since Baruch was highly involved in the synagogue and frequented the Temple, he had felt the disparity. It wasn't getting easier, it was getting more difficult as time went on. Whenever Jesus did something that went against the Pharisees, the repercussions were felt throughout the nation.

The family had meetings every now and then, especially when something controversial happened. The discussions about the Sabbath were intense. Discussions about the law being fulfilled in Jesus had gotten downright argumentative, until Baruch broke in with his understanding that the Messiah was not there to be a political figure, but a suffering one. Wasn't the Messiah the Son? Wasn't he to be the one to bring salvation, unlike anything they had seen before? They had prayed together to have peace and God's direction. How could anyone do these things unless God was with him? Baruch would end the discussions with the affirmation, "He raised the dead!" No one was able to argue with that. They had to trust God had a plan.

Time went on. Jesus had come to Jerusalem a couple of times. Elihu couldn't take it anymore. He had to see for himself. He went to Shimei to talk about it.

"I know we are busy right now, but when aren't we? Is there a way for me to go listen to Jesus while he is here?"

With a knowing look and little snicker, Shimei said, "I knew this would come. I just didn't know when it would break. You know you are my best weaver, no one does what you do on the loom."

"Thank you. I am trying to teach Isaac and Ezra, but with all the orders, it is hard to teach and get it done at the same time. We have only one high-quality loom. There isn't enough time to let them play and make mistakes. I am too busy making the cloth you've had ordered. Maybe we should look into getting another. We have the work, let's think about the future."

"You're right. Tell you what. I will order another. When it is set up and functional, you can take the time you want."

"No, I will miss the timing. Why don't you order it made and I will take a couple of days to set it up? I just can't do the work I really want to do. I'm a little distracted and growing weary. Give me the time. It will be better for the business in the long run."

Shimei knew he wasn't going to win this one. He was losing the heart of his best weaver. He needed to get him some satisfaction. "Okay. When and for how long?"

"I heard that his friends in Bethany had called for him. The brother is sick. They called for Jesus to come heal him. He will probably come for that. I will keep an eye and ear open. When I know he is coming, I will go then. Does that seem reasonable? Until then, I will start figuring out how to rearrange the shop for another loom."

Knowing he was outmaneuvered, Shimei could only smile and resolve himself to the inevitable. "Sounds good. I'll send word to the carpenter today." Shimei knew how to take care of his people. He knew where his strengths were and where his weaknesses stood. He knew that if he worked with Elihu, it would all get done and done well. This is what made things work. They all worked together to make things functional. It was working well so far.

Bethany was only a mile and a half away from Jerusalem to the east, on the eastern slopes of the Mount of Olives. Elihu had heard that Jesus was on the way. It didn't come through official channels, but the common folk who watched the roads.

He had met the siblings who ministered to the needs of Jesus and his disciples before. They weren't wealthy exactly, but they were well off. There were two sisters and a younger brother. Martha, the oldest and the one in charge over their estate; Mary, the younger sister; and Lazarus lived in a good house in Bethany. They had established a relationship with Jesus near the beginning of his ministry. Having a large house, they could accommodate all of them fairly easily. When the brother got sick, they sent word to Jesus to come help, but he hadn't come quickly enough. As Elihu found out when he came, the brother had actually died. The whole town was upset. Being of the stature in the community as they were, this news was devastating to all of them. They had buried him in a tomb on the hill of their property just outside of town.

Elihu didn't want to waste his time away from the shop, so he waited. Word was that Jesus had left the place where he had been staying to make his way here. He sure was taking his time.

Righteous Sheol was in a state of continual disruption. News of what was happening above in the land of the living was trickling in as people died who had seen, heard or even experienced miracles. One of the greatest disruptions came when a man named John came. He was the one God had sent to be the forerunner for the Messiah. He was himself the fulfillment of scripture, which made him quite a celebrity here.

His story was amazing, but to one, in particular, it was astronomical! Malachi had been used of the Spirit to write about this one who was to come before the Messiah. Hearing how what he had written had come to pass, and the details of how that worked, was a dream come true for Malachi. He had become a near constant companion to John. When all heard that he had been beheaded, however, the atmosphere got a little more serious. When John found his parents, the family reunion was spectacular. Details of all this reverberated throughout Sheol.

Then a new man came. This new arrival was causing excitement that even rivaled the news Shimon brought so long ago and the coming of John. A young man had come who had known the Messiah personally! There had been others who brought reports of what was happening, but nothing like this! This man was Jesus's friend.

When he came in, he was disoriented and confused. Like so many who didn't think it was time for them to die, he was in great denial. As he got used to where he was, he was brought to the elders because of his news. Shimon and Malachi were there when he was brought in. His escort was really excited, bringing him in probably before he should have been, being very unsure about everything.

"Father Abraham! You have to hear this. This is Lazarus from Bethany. He has quite a story to tell. I will let him tell you." The escort motioned for him to speak to the Elders, giving him some encouragement, bowing, and backing away.

Lazarus looked frightened and bewildered, trying to understand what was happening all around him. Finally, he focused on the man standing in front of him with the long white beard. "Abraham? Like, THE Abraham? Father of Israel? I... I don't..."

Abraham stepped forward, gently putting his hand on Lazarus's shoulder, looking him deeply in the eyes. "Peace." He let that start to sink in, working at dispelling the feeling of being overwhelmed. "Peace. You are safe. There is nothing to worry about. Take your time. Do you have any questions first?"

"I was sick with a severe fever. We were waiting for Jesus to come to heal me. He was our hope. I can't have died. Jesus was coming!"

"I know you don't understand what is happening, but none of us really do," Abraham comforted him. "None of us pick the time of our death. It never feels right. We have to trust in our God to know when things are the best and why. You are here. That isn't disputed. Jehovah God has a plan and a purpose. It is always greater than we can comprehend. Relax. All will be made known in time."

Looking into the eyes of Abraham calmed the young man. He relaxed. "But why didn't he come?"

"That isn't for you to know right now. We are in His hands and can trust Him. All you need to do right now is embrace your condition and this place. It will make things easier for you and those around you. Please, sit with me."

"We can sit? On what?" His eyes were starting to get used to the things in this realm. What looked like rocks appeared with some trees and grass. Abraham sat, showing him it was okay to sit. Lazarus stepped around the rock and sat on it. It didn't feel like a rock, but it was firm and not uncomfortable. "This is all so different," he thought. But when he looked at Abraham, he was able to trust and relax.

Shimon had felt what he was feeling. It actually almost made him laugh. He walked over and sat opposite Lazarus. Malachi snickered and joined them. There was quite a crowd around them. Some of them were prophets and kings of old. They had been gathering more and more since word of the Messiah had come, and now that he had started his public presence, many wanted to be the first to hear reports.

Shimon looked around. He had only been here a little over thirty years according to the reports that he had heard about the date up above. Time was tricky. There was no sun or moon, no one slept. No one was fatigued. They just were and continued to be. Now, however, with the reports of the Messiah and what he was doing, all the ages seemed to be coming to a completion.

There was King David. He was really fun to talk to. He would break out into song and dance at any reason to praise God. He really missed King Solomon. His moving into idolatry was devastating and had set things up for the other kings who followed. Hosea, Hezekiah and couple of other kings had been godly, but that was it. The prophets were much greater in representation. They had fun getting together. Piecing history together was a hobby of theirs. Malachi was the last of them until John showed up. Priests were there in number. There were many exceptions, but for the most part, the priests were godly. Along with all of them were their families. There was no pretention. All of them were just normal folk. They had been used of God and now were waiting for all things to be done.

What was interesting to all of them is how little importance they had here. You could be talking to a man and suddenly realize you were talking to Moses and Aaron. They were just as interested in your life as you were of theirs.

Now everyone wanted to hear about Jesus. Lazarus wasn't what was important; it was his news that caught attention. Everyone was interested in what he said Jesus said and did. John had told how Jesus had answered the question of whether he was the One or if there would be another, with the answer, "The blind see, the lame walk, the lepers cleansed, the deaf hear, the dead are raised, and the gospel is given to the poor." That was the badge of office for the Messiah. That is why they all hung on every word Lazarus had to say.

Abraham had a way about him that made people relax. He could get folks talking without them realizing how much they had told. Once you got started, it seemed just to flow. Lazarus fell into that category. Abraham got him talking about how they met Jesus and how they had become friends. Lazarus had accompanied Jesus on his forays into Jerusalem. He had seen the miracles and heard the sermons and teachings. All of it rolled off his tongue to the pleasure and delight of this august audience. There was one thing that stood out among it all.

"What was it like to have Jesus and the disciples around? What did they talk about?"

"They mostly talked about what had happened and where they were going next. The disciples didn't seem to know much. All of the teachings were thick of meaning, and most of the time none of us really knew what he was talking about. We knew there were deeper meanings than we could possibly understand. He told us that the Holy Spirit would reveal things to us and remind us of what was said. I think he mostly meant the disciples. They were being groomed for ministry in ways they definitely didn't comprehend. They don't know anything about here, that's for sure."

"Did Jesus tell of the plans for the future?"

"Oh, yes! Again, we didn't get what he was talking about. It was draped in mystery with clues we don't have yet. That was much of our discussions when Jesus wasn't around. 'What did he mean by this?' or 'Did you understand about the fig tree?' That was a constant source of discussion. Especially when he talked about the near future. He told us he was going to die."

That struck much harder than Lazarus had intended. Abraham's mouth fell open in a look of astonishment. "He said what?"

"He said he was going to be crucified. He told us all not to worry. Everything was going according to plan. He said he didn't come to be served, but to serve and to give his soul as a ransom for many." Lazarus looked around him. Everyone was stunned. It looked like all the air had been sucked out of the place. He didn't understand what was going on.

"This is truly a deep piece of news. We will have to discuss this." Abraham had effectively shut off the conversation. "Thank you, Lazarus. You have been most gracious in telling us all these things. I know you have much to process about being here. We have much to process because of what you have told us. You are welcome to talk to me any time you wish, but for now, it is probably best for you to gain understanding of where you are." Abraham stood, bowed respectfully, and walked away after nodding to Lazarus's escort to continue.

Shimon stood and walked after Abraham. "Abraham! A moment please?" Abraham stopped and turned to face Shimon. "This is what I have been trying to tell you. Jesus is here as the suffering Messiah, not the reigning Messiah. He has got to go through this first. What was told to Isaiah and David are prophecies of great truth. Yes, he is healing and doing all the miracles, but it won't stop the leaders from hating him."

With his head dropping, showing the heaviness of his thoughts, Abraham responded with a sigh. "I hear what you are saying. It does look like that is the direction it is taking. The ramifications are dire, don't you think?"

"Well, yes. But the outcome will be worth it! What is our Messiah going to do and what is being done for the world? We must believe that Yawveh has a plan and knows what is needed."

Raising his head to look Shimon in the face, Abraham was yielding to the debate. It was no longer a theory. This was as practical as it got. The Messiah was doing something even deeper than they had thought. And now they had proof in the form of one who had heard it from Jesus's own mouth. "Let's convene the elders. We need to settle this."

It took a while to catch up with Malachi, not knowing which way they all went. It was important to Shimon to talk this out more. When all else failed, he knew he could find him with his family. It was how they all sorted things out. They would have in-depth discussions and then spend time with family to process things. Shimon did that, too. He spent time with Rebekah and Joanna; he even found his parents. However, talking things out seemed to work best for him.

Malachi was with his wife and sons. They were an intense group. Living with a prophet all those years took a certain kind of person. They were loving, but strong. Malachi had been dead for over four hundred years. He had several people he knew and loved, many he met here. Shimon was one of them. Shimon knew them all and was always accepted and wanted for fellowship. He really liked being with them, but this time was different. He wanted Malachi alone.

Coming up to the group, he greeted them all warmly. Uncharacteristically, though, he went straight to Malachi. "May I talk with you for a while?" His concern gave Malachi concern.

"Sure. Is everything all right?"

Walking away for a distance, Shimon started slowly, not really knowing how to start or where he headed with this conversation; he just needed to talk. "All my life I have been pursuing the Messiah. While alive, it was the one major topic of my studies. I even taught my children not to expect a Messianic ruler on a throne, but one that would walk among us as one of us and suffer. I was never sure how, but with Lazarus coming, I'm convinced of his crucifixion. With him having power over life and death, it took my studies to another depth. What if they can't kill him?" He checked himself there. "No, that isn't right. He said he would die. There has got to be something that is beyond what we have seen."

Shimon was talking, but Malachi knew he wasn't talking to him necessarily. It was deep thought, but Malachi was having fun watching his friend dive into this subject like nothing he had seen him do before, even with all the discussions they'd had.

"You are missing the point," Malachi said to bring things back into perspective. That rattled Shimon out of his thoughts and jerked his attention back to his friend. He looked up quizzically at Malachi almost as if he had slapped him. "You forget why we are here. We aren't here to solve these mysteries. Our conclusions don't matter much. Our biggest job is to learn and trust in Yawveh. He has a plan. We do not have a big part in that plan any longer. Those who are alive do. Don't try to solve the mystery. Revel in it. Enjoy it. Go ahead and dig deeply, but keep your trust in our God knowing we haven't been given all the information yet. Yawveh isn't bound to tell us everything. He hasn't before and is only giving us pieces now. Let Him perform what He is doing."

It was closer to a slap than he thought. It shook Shimon deeply. "You are right. I am trying to do what I did while alive. Things are different now. We have to let things unfold. We have been given the best place to view the hand of God of all times." The knowledge hit Shimon like an explosion in his mind. He grabbed Malachi by both arms pulling him close as his face beamed the joy he was feeling. "I understand! I've been going at this all wrong. Thank you! Thank you so dearly! You are the best friend a person could ever hope for. I bless you!"

It was all Shimon could do to not burst forth in dancing. Malachi just stood there wide-eyed and laughing, not knowing what to expect from Shimon right now. "Good. I'm glad you got it!"

"Now what I need is more information. There is nothing I can do about it, but I can be the best spectator God needs me to be!" Then it occurred to him, "I have someone here that knows things more than anyone before. I need to go listen."

"Maybe I had better come with you to keep you out of trouble."

"Oh, will you? That would be wonderful! Let's go find Lazarus."

They had spent much time together, helping Lazarus orient to the new environment and getting his mindset working. Shimon started feeling like he had known Jesus all his life as the stories unfolded. He could see the fulfillment of scriptural prophecies and the joy of seeing God's hand in all that had happened in the Torah, the Psalms, and the Prophets. They took Lazarus to several of the prophets and let them tell what they had written and how it felt to them. Shimon felt like this was a party to have fun in, he hadn't had such joy in his life. Since time was unregistered, they had no idea how long they had been talking. With a person such as Lazarus in their midst, they were interrupted often as people came to meet him and ask questions.

At one point, Shimon introduced Lazarus to another Lazarus. It was impressive to Lazarus from Bethany that a former beggar like Lazarus from Jerusalem had the same importance as the elders. All came here with nothing to offer, just the faith they had in Jehovah of Hosts. There was no hierarchy or position of status. They both were impressed when they met Lazarus the High Priest, son of Aaron. It caused a bond between them that caused them all to laugh. They were all so different, but their commonality was their faith and trust in the Lord God of Israel.

"I never knew this kind of life existed," Lazarus stated at one point. "We always think of death as bad, don't we?"

"Well, it is for those who don't know Yawveh. Remember how much it talks about the difference between life and death, good and evil, blessing and cursing. Remember how much Psalms and Proverbs talk about the difference between being wise and being foolish and the outcome." Malachi got quite talkative when inspired. He was actually poetic at times. Shimon always enjoyed it when he got this way.

It caused Lazarus to be more introspective. "I really love being here. There is so much to learn. However, it makes me wonder what is happening back at home. My sisters would be so sad since I died. I really wonder what Jesus is up to and what is happening with him."

The atmosphere of Bethany was somber at best. Lazarus had been put in the family tomb. The mourning had continued for days. Because they were people of status in the community, practically everyone in town was involved. Martha tried to put a pragmatic face on it all. The mourners really bothered her; they were unnecessary. She really wanted to be left alone. She wanted Jesus to come and set things in order.

Jesus had been told of Lazarus's sickness but had decided to stay beyond the Jordan. The disciples had thought it was because of fear of the Pharisees and Priests who were speaking threats. They were certainly afraid, but Jesus had a different attitude. He actually waited for some reason. He told them Lazarus was sleeping and it was time to go wake him up. They thought that was good, Lazarus would be getting better if he was sleeping. Then Jesus told them Lazarus was dead. That depressed the whole crew. Jesus still told them he was going to him. They didn't get it.

He had traveled the distance with a group of men that were depressed about Lazarus, he being the only one with a positive attitude, which baffled the disciples. Shouldn't he be sad at the death of his friend?

Elihu heard he was close and went out to be there when he got close. There were many who had gathered around Jesus as he traveled. Elihu just joined the crowd, but he stayed close to hear what Jesus would have to say.

Coming close to Bethany, Martha was told he was coming. Jesus didn't come to the house, but stayed on the road. He was at the intersection from the house to the tomb. He wanted to go there. Martha came out to greet him and welcome him to her home. Seeing him again filled her with joy. She knew something was going to happen, but her faith had wavered. She ran up to him seizing the hand he held out to her. She looked imploringly into his eyes as she spoke.

"Lord," she said, "if you were here my brother would not have died. But even now I know that as many things as you may ask God, God will give you."

"Your brother will rise again."

"I know that he will rise again in the resurrection on the last day." She was trying to keep her hope in check by saying the proper thing.

Jesus spoke to her gently and knowingly. "I am the resurrection and the life. The one believing into me, though he die, he shall live. And everyone living and believing into me shall not die to the age, not ever! Do you believe this?"

"Yes, Lord, I have believed that you are the Messiah, the son of God who comes into the world."

Martha bowed under the scrutiny. "Please, stay here. I will return." Turning she ran toward the house. Her mind was racing about what was just said. Could there be hope still? Could she allow herself to think that way?

Coming into the house, she saw and heard the mourners. Some of them were professional mourners, paid to wail. It was part of the culture to show prestige and social rank. They had been hired by the town council. Martha tried to ignore them as much as possible. She finally found Mary, surrounded by these people. Martha came to where she sat and kneeling in front of her, she got her attention by putting her hands on Mary's knees. As Mary looked at her sister inquisitively, Martha whispered so no one else could hear her, "The Teacher is here and calls you."

Mary gasped in surprise and jumped up. Without waiting for anyone, she quickly walked out of the room and out the door. The mourners and friends that were in the house were surprised at this sudden jump. They noted that she was probably going to the tomb to weep and had best follow and join her. The crowd fairly kept Martha from keeping up with her sister, so she followed as she could.

Mary saw Jesus at the crossroads and ran up to him. Enveloped in grief, she fell at his feet weeping. In the sobs, she cried out, "Lord, if you were here, my brother would not have died!" Her tone was filled with emotion and accusation.

Jesus heard her and saw her deep weeping. He felt the complete lack of faith in those statements. Then looking up he saw the mourners and people coming with her and the complete unbelief they were carrying. He had come to do something great, but they were all filled with doubt, sorrow, fear, and despair. It overwhelmed Jesus who let out a great groan of frustration. He had to steel himself for the fight at hand. "Where have you put him?" His tone was one of authority and demand. It took Mary by surprise, causing her to rock back on her heels and look up at him.

One nearby said, "Lord, come this way and see." Martha came up and helped Mary stand as Jesus started following the one who had spoken. His emotion was now coming strongly to the front. He began to weep, but the attitude of anger was still showing. It was hard to guess what he was angry about. The air was filled with deep emotion.

Elihu was keeping close to Jesus. He watched all this happen. The man standing next to him said, "See how he loved him!" Elihu looked at the man quizzically. He wondered to himself, "Do you understand anything that is truly happening here?" As he thought that, another one close by said, "Was he, the one opening the eyes of the blind one, not able to have caused that this one should not die?"

Jesus looked at the man, and the frustration again was more than he could hold back. He nearly snorted in anger at the piles of unbelief he had to deal with here. Elihu was seeing and feeling it all. This was incredibly powerful. He could see that the vast majority of people had no idea what was going on, but thought they did.

Coming to the tomb, Jesus saw it was a cave with a stone lying on it. "Lift the stone," Jesus commanded.

Martha spoke up. "Lord, he already smells bad, for it has been four days."

Jesus, turned facing her. "Did I not say to you that if you would believe you will see the glory of God?" Looking over at the men standing there, they got the message. Elihu joined them as it took many men to lift the stone and put it off to the side. Standing in front of the tomb, Y'shau looked upward and said loudly, "Father, I thank you that you heard me. And I know that you always hear me, but because of the crowd standing around, I said it, that they might believe that you sent me!"

Then focusing his gaze into the tomb, Jesus cried out with a loud voice, "Lazarus! Here! Outside!"

They were discussing how life was working in Sheol and how peaceful it was, when suddenly they all heard a very loud voice. "Lazarus!" Lazarus knew it was talking to him. The look on his face was total astonishment. Everyone was looking at him. No one knew what was happening; it caught them all by surprise.

"Here!" Lazarus felt himself start to rise. They all were watching with intense interest.

"Outside!" With a simple glance as his last act there, Lazarus shot up and was gone in an instant. Everyone there was stunned. No one said anything for a minute. "What was that all about?" Shimon looked at the person standing next to him who had just spoken. Shimon knew. He had seen this before.

Lazarus found himself not able to see, but he was in a dark, confined space. His body was bound up and it was hard to move. Body? Where he was laying was hard and uncomfortable. The air was musty and hard to breath. Something was wrapped around his head. His legs started to fall off the edge of what he was laying on. He had a real urge to stand up. Unseen hands helped him stand and led him to hobble in a certain direction. He had to hop shuffle. Progress was slow. Understanding was not coming. He didn't know help from angels made this possible, but the King had spoken, things were ordered.

He could faintly see some light coming through the cloth around his head. Though diffused, it gave him some direction. He could hear people ahead of him. He was yelling for help, but his voice was completely muffled. He just kept moving as best he could.

He heard Jesus tell people, "Loose him. Let him go." The people were stunned seeing the dead coming out of the tomb, so no one was moving. Jesus's words jolted them into action. Elihu jumped in grabbing the cloth around his head so he could breathe and see. The first person Lazarus saw was the grandson of the man he had just left, though he couldn't put that together. Lazarus's mind was confused. The only thing he remembered was being sick; he didn't retain anything that had transpired the last four days. It was only distant thoughts and the feeling of a dream he had. Every now and then a part of a memory sparked through, but not enough to hold onto.

What he did understand, though, was that he had died and Jesus had raised him from the dead. He was no longer sick; he had been healed in the rising.

It was Elihu who was changed, though. He had just witnessed something beyond anything he could have imagined before. His faith soared. He could see the power of the Messiah and why he did what he was doing. He would go home and make sure they were supporters for Jesus and his mission. What he really took away from this experience was the value of faith and the damage of unbelief.

He also saw the reactions of the people around him. Some were absolutely thrilled, praising God. Others were confused as to what really happened. However, there were many who were angry. The Pharisees and the Priesthood felt that Jesus was flaunting things in their faces. He wasn't yielding to their religious authority. He could do things they couldn't do and it made them look bad. He had taught things that went against their teachings. He had called them vipers and sepulchers. This was pushing them to respond. The future was charged with conflict.

No one was seeing what else was happening around them. The dark realm was also stirred up beyond history. Having two raised from the dead after a few hours or even minutes was hard for the demons to handle. Satan himself was getting involved in Jesus's activities. All the demons around him were on edge. Satan hated Jesus beyond anyone they had ever known. He couldn't stop Jesus from doing anything. He was taking people away from the darkness and giving them all hope. Satan had no clear idea what to do about him; he just wanted him dead. The religious leaders were firmly in his pocket, but they were limited in what they could do. All the demons were on edge and flighty.

The departed spirits had no authority, nor even a plan. All they wanted was to experience the addictions. They were evil, but they had no ability to make anything work. They needed the demons to stir things up. The departed spirits were, however, spectators to the greatest confrontation of good and evil. The ones addicted to violence were hungry and in full anticipation. The others didn't know how this was going to work for them. When the demons were excited, it filled them all with a twisted form of hope for them to be slightly fulfilled in their drives. None of them could see the outcome nor the way to work things. There was confusion in the ranks.

Demons and departed spirits alike were found around tombs. However, there were more around this one. The death of Lazarus was a victory for them. For some reason, the friend of Jesus was open to disease. The spirits worked hard at trying to kill him. This would show that the realm of darkness had power. They could get through to one who was close to the Son of God! That was promising.

Satan stood at a distance and watched. They were still limited in who they could touch and how. But knowing they were touching this one was thrilling to him. Then word came that Jesus was coming. The demons couldn't get too close to the band of disciples, especially when they were close to Jesus. They could, however, keep an eye on him from afar. They kept Satan informed. Now there would be a victory to rub in the face of the Messiah.

As Jesus entered the village, it opened the ranks of the spirits before him. It was getting more difficult to wreak havoc when Jesus was around. His light was continually beaming into the spirit realm making it hard to work in the darkness. They were working on bringing fear to everyone. Fear and doubt were the main weapons they could employ. They had been implanting doubt in the mind of Martha for a while now, ever since her brother was sick and they couldn't seem to get ahold of Jesus. Mary was a lot easier because of her emotional state. The crowd who came to mourn were already in their pockets. They had been able to plant some doubt in the disciples, but it was tricky being that close to the Word himself.

Then Jesus came. While he talked with Martha, they knew they were losing a little ground, but when Mary came and was accompanied by all the religious people, the doubt was thick and delicious. Then Jesus got upset. He groaned at the unbelief. His faith beamed out from him like an explosion. Had they overplayed their hand? Jesus seemed to understand what they had been doing. He knew what he was fighting. Satan became a little nervous.

They all went up the hill to the tomb. The demons were feeding doubt and unbelief to all who were close. They worked on the religious ones around them. Maybe their doubt and unbelief could keep Jesus from doing anything. It had worked in Nazareth. Hopefully, it would work here.

Jesus groaned again. His fervency was becoming intense. By the time he reached the tomb, he was positively beaming faith all around him. Then he spoke with an authority that shook the entire realm. He called to the dead man! He commanded him to come back! Instantly a shaft of light shot down into the ground through the tomb from above it. The spirits below it were dispersed from around it. There was a completely free channel. The spirit of the dead man came up from Sheol and blasted into his body. A burst of light came out of his body, and his body was totally healed.

Every spirit was stunned, including Satan. They all recoiled, falling back. The aura of doubt and fear they had been feeding for so long now, was negated and replaced with faith that caused pain in the demonic realm. Spirits were sent running away, completely out of control.

Satan left, needing to regroup and think about the plans they had for the future. He was nearing a panic. The only thing he could think of for now was to try to get a conspiracy to kill Lazarus again. As long as he was alive, he would remind everyone of the power of Jesus. This wasn't good. Would Jesus just raise him again? Was he now impervious to death? He put the religious spirits right to work on the religious leaders to kill Lazarus but he knew that plan was doomed to fail.

There was nothing but turmoil in his mind and reign. The principalities and demonic rulers were no good. There was no cohesion, just confusion. And fear. There was great fear in the dark realm now. Their greatest plan had failed most miserably. Now what?

Satan raged. He fumed. He spat vehement slurs at everything. He hadn't felt this helpless since they were cast out of heaven. He needed a plan and he needed it now.

A thought struck him. If Jesus was going to raise those they killed, then that was futile. But what if they killed Jesus? There was no one to raise Him. Killing the one who raised people would leave no one to do the raising!

Brilliant! His focus returned as he started seeing the possibilities. Darkness got darker. Satan bought the plan completely. He gathered his hierarchy, fiercely demanding attention and obedience. He had always wanted to kill Jesus, but now it became his entire evil focus.

The story continues in Book Two

About The Author

Lee Eddy is a Bible teacher with over 50 years of experience, including pastor, missionary, seminar leader, and ministry developer. His ministry, Face to Face Healing Ministry, as set many free from addictions and interpersonal damage. He has written several teaching books and manuals including the Great Romance Marriage Course, Rocksot Teaching course, Pure Man course, and Advance Pure Man. With his wife of 46 years, Roxanne, he has raised 3 children. They live in Colorado and are continuing using and developing ways of bringing others into freedom.

The Weaving of Threads

Excerpts from Book 2

Sheol was next to pandemonium, if that were possible. Lazarus had been raised. They all heard the voice that called him out. What did this mean? How did it happen? Speculation was rampant. To souls who had been dead for some time, some of them for thousands of years, to see someone so blatantly raised caused many to be amazed and perplexed. The angels ministered to them for peace, and that helped. The elders convened, trying to bring some semblance of understanding. The discussions were not that deep considering no one knew any more than anyone else.

Malachi brought the point he had told Shimon earlier that they were only to observe and not do anything. It seemed to make sense, and things were calmed a bit. Shimon had the same question in his mind that many did: if someone can be raised, can we? The question would go unanswered because no one knew. There was no way to know.

Finally, they came to the consensus that the only thing to do was trust God, praise Him, wait, and see. Life returned to whatever could be called normal, except the thought was still in their minds.

Things were starting to get interesting among the living. The Jewish religious and political leaders were trying to come up with plans to kill Jesus. They were being fueled by the Dark Spiritual realm. Satan and his creepy horde were working feverishly to stir up these sentiments. Jesus was a threat to the Jewish leaders lifestyles, incomes, power, and prestige. The problem was, though, the people loved Jesus and considered him a prophet of God.

Everywhere you went, there were discussions about Him. The people who believed were solid in their belief, but they were a definite minority. Most of the common people would go with whatever made their lives easier. There were some who wanted to use Jesus for their own political purposes to stir the people up to rebellion against the Romans. One thing was certain: something was about to happen.

The realm of the demons was extremely busy. They were going all over the place stirring up people in every way they could. The demons would employ the departed spirits of violence and disruption. The demons would get people all worked up until their soul would be open to being inhabited by a departed spirit that would stay and irritate the souls they inhabited. Even the departed spirits like Lachish were used to help get people desiring the alcohol more than usual. The spiritual atmosphere was charged with evil intent.

For the most part, the demons had full reign to do whatever they wished. It was like a party where everyone did what they wanted. There was chaos in the air in Jerusalem. The greatest activity was around wherever Jesus went. It was like the demonic realm was looking for ways to get in and destroy this man. They were swarming around in anticipation of something.

Something masked Jesus from their prying eyes this night. They were left out, swirling around trying to find him. The only thing they knew for sure was that Satan was close to him. They counted on that.

Lee E. Eddy